Nikki Gemmell's othe
The Bride Stripped Bar
now lives in London.

A NOVEL

SHIVER

NIKKI GEMMELL

Australian Government

Books Alive is an Australian Government
initiative developed through the Australia Council

A Vintage Book
Published by
Random House Australia Pty Ltd
20 Alfred Street, Milsons Point, NSW 2061
http://www.randomhouse.com.au

Sydney New York Toronto
London Auckland Johannesburg
and agencies throughout the world

First published in 1997
Reprinted 1997, 1999, 2001, 2003, 2004
Copyright © Nikki Gemmell 1997

National Library of Australia
Cataloguing-in-Publication Data

Gemmell, Nikki
 Shiver: a novel

 2nd ed.
 ISBN 1 74051 324 X.

 I. Title.

 A823.3

Design by Yolande Gray
Typeset by DOCUPRO, Sydney
Printed and bound by the McPherson's Printing Group, Maryborough, Victoria

For Martin

ACKNOWLEDGEMENTS

Thank you to the people of the Antarctic Division who made possible my fifty-day voyage, which gave me the idea to write a novel set in Antarctica.

Thanks also to Jane Palfreyman at Random House, and to Alison Angles, Chris Doran, Craig James, Lizzie Foschia, Alison Ray, Andrew Sholl and my family for their love and support and wisdom.

And finally, thank you to Alison French for her encouragement right from the start, her editorial energy, and the loan of her house.

'Beyond this point, there be dragons . . .'

The advice on the extremities
of ancient maps, signalling the
end of the known world.

CONTENTS

*T*hey put me into a small, white, still room and that was wrong. One day Rick came and took me outside into air that was vivid with smell and colour and noise. I told him where I had to go. He drove me away with a honk of the horn and at a service station on the rim of the city we stopped and swapped places and I drove on. I turned up the music and wound down the window and held out my hand, butting the breeze. I drove deep into the nights until we came to the desert.

I'm here because Antarctica has given me a taste for deserts. The meanest motherfucking desert of them all has given me an addiction for wide lands and tall skies and air that hums. It's a furious need; it's under my skin and it isn't going to let me go. I lie in my swag in this other desert, sharply awake. The wind has blown all night, blowing away sleep. I'm writing about Antarctica, by torch-

1

light, on my belly. Just like I used to lie on my belly on the ice.

Heat comes ahead of the day. I flick off my torch, flip onto my back and listen to the Central Australian sky.

There's a hum of stillness. It's as though there's a bowl over my head. There's the last star, the first bird and flies, before six.

I flick them away. Then in thickening heat ants begin a speedy traverse of my skin. I feel like Gulliver. My hand slaps and sweeps at my thighs and hipbones and wrists and I stand up quickly from my swag and the Antarctica pages scatter. It's almost day.

Rick's made a fire. Burning sticks crack strongly into the stillness. He hands me a tin mug of milky tea. The liquid's lifted the soft red dust from the cup's sides, lifted it like cinnamon to the surface.

I tell Rick I didn't sleep and he says Antarctica again and I say yeah. He worries the fire with a stick.

There's a high gathering of clouds. There's the smell of wet on the wind. A storm rumbles in the wings of the sky; it's as though a huge table is being dragged across the floor of heaven.

In a controlled rush we clear things away. I scrub our tin plates with water and desert sand. When I'm nearly through, I look up and stop.

The sky hangs. The birds have hushed. There's a blanket of stillness, as if the whole world is poised, waiting for the storm. The strange yellow light ahead of the rain brings out vividly the colours around us—the ochres, the browns, the bleached greens. I think of the strict Antarctic palette of white and blue and grey and black. Bellies of pink arc above us as Major Mitchells swoop by in a sudden evacuation. The smell of eucalyptus is flint sharp in the air. I look across at Rick. He's kicking sand over the grey remains of the fire. I think of snow being kicked over the carcass of a day-old seal.

Antarctica is seared like acid on my mind.

I can never go back. I don't reckon it's meant for humans. I tell this to Rick. He says nothing. I know he thinks I'm here because I'm running away, as far away as I can get.

The first fat splats of rain come. One hits me like a nail. The earth opens up as if it's breathing.

We run. I take down my towel from the dead branch of the tree and snag a splinter in my finger. I can't get it out. We run to the cabin of the four wheel drive and slam the heavy doors. Rick takes my hand in his and opens it flat and my palm is a road map of ochre lines. He tells me to hold still and with his two dirty blunt thumbnails he squeezes and stops and squeezes again and gently, the sliver pops up and out. I'm still and quiet because I'm crying. Because of Antarctica. Because of something I'd forgotten.

A blowy howly mongrel of a day and there was the grit from the wind and a shard of something in my eye, the sudden sharp pain of it and the scream, I can't see! and he was at me swiftly and peering and holding my head braced tight between his big bear hands and yelling, Hold still! and he was licking my eyeball while I was kicking and squealing like a pony, he was licking and licking until the speck was gone and I came up blinking and smiling and still.

I can catalogue Antarctica by touch.

The touch of air sucked dry on my cheek, the fur of a day-old seal pup, the touch of an iceberg, a blizzard, a lover, the touch of sweat at minus twenty-three, of a camera stuck to the skin on my face, of cold like glass cutting into my skin, of a snowflake, of a dead man, of a doctor's fingers on my inner thigh, of a tongue on my eye.

ONE

GALLOPING

DAYS

It begins with touch, in Sydney.

A finger's up my bum. The finger's male. It's brisk in a sheath of powdered white latex that seems as thin as skin. I'm naked from the waist down, on my side on a government surgical bed. The mattress is meanly thin. My body's curled foetally, bunched like a fist to the wall.

Doctor Pat Pisano says he's feeling for bowel cancer. I didn't think I was in the risk category. A loud blush is gatecrashing my face and Doctor Pat Pisano can see it. I went to primary school with him. It's one of those excruciating coincidences. I haven't seen him for fifteen years. He asks me if I'm married yet and I tell him I'm not. All he had to do was look at my left hand. I look at his. He tells me I'm the only person going on the voyage who doesn't have to be examined by the government psychiatrist and he says little do they know, with a high giggle. I never liked him at school.

His fingers and the fingers of eleven other medical practitioners are thorough as they roam my body, searching for abnormalities that will prevent me from going to Antarctica. Specimens have to be fit and I'm not sure I'm going to pass. The fingers are thorough and gentle and firm as they attach electrodes to my arms and legs and chest to measure my heart rate, guide my torso in front of the x-ray machine, probe my wide-open mouth, take my urine in warm plastic cups, pinch skin.

I pass the medical. There's one query in the doctor's report faxed to my work. SLIGHT BUILD, QUESTION MARK.

'Does this mean you're going to freeze quicker?' says Lyn, the chief of staff, as she hands over the report.

4.03 a.m. A new day at work. The desk's bare, the streets are lean. The newsroom's stilled, waiting for the onslaught.

The police scanner coughs, scratches. I lean forward to listen. Domestic. Tic tic. Stabbing. Tic tic. MVA. Torana into pole. One to Westmead, serious. One minor, treated at scene. Yeah yeah I'll pick up a Maccers on the way, two filet-os and a pinkshake yeah yeah. Some dude singing 'Somewhere Over The Rainbow' and 'Not in the Mood'. Ah cops. Tic tic. Nothing doing. Tic tic.

The city's smug, asleep.

10 a.m. The airwaves are crowded. Domestic MVA stabbing assault domestic domestic. L-plater, failed to stop, old lady run over. Driver distress. A zip-up bag at a Blacktown bus stand dripping blood. Unconfirmed, can't be found. A woman threatening suicide on a city-bound bus. A brawl at a mall.

'Lyn,' I say, 'It's dead. Any stories?'

She slaps a press release on my desk. Global warming. An international conference.

'Good practice, my love,' she says. 'And by the way, how many cocks did you have to suck to get this little gig in the ice anyway?'

I smack my lips and grin. 'Too bloody many.'

None. The newsroom was offered an Antarctic trip by the Australian government and I put up my hand and was chosen. One journo a year, on average, gets to go. It's good PR for the government, it helps in publicising and demystifying the nation's presence on the ice. The newsroom jumped at the offer and so did I. The voyage gets me off the police round which I suspect I'm too good at because I've been stuck with it for too long. And it gets me off the morning shift.

I ring the number on the press release. The talent's good. She says last summer the hole over Antarctica was the size of Europe. Good grab. She says each year the hole's getting bigger. Great stuff. When the tape's turned off at the end of it I tell her I'm just about to go down there. She's the first woman I've spoken to who's been. I ask her what it's like. She says for a start there aren't many women. She says that on the Antarctic stations everything I do will be watched, from talking with a man to drinking at the bar to eating in the mess. She says a woman's attention is sought persistently.

I tell her I think I'm going to like that a lot and she says, suddenly fierce, that after a while the attention's utterly exhausting and she wouldn't wish it on anyone.

'And if it gets to the stage of actually working out a way of sleeping with someone, well, you have to be incredibly discreet. Most people haven't been touched for a very long time and they don't want to see the people who are getting it, flouting it.'

She's warning me. She wishes me a crisp good luck and hangs up.

Midday. Knock-off time. Lyn yells goodbye and asks what's the ratio of men to women, down at that place I'm going to. I tell her there are very few women and a lot of beards and that touching is taboo.

'Well that'll be a challenge then.' We laugh. 'Hooroo.'

My body's too tired to do the twenty minute walk to my flat. I get the train home to dinner and bed.

A man called Jim rings in the thick of work. I'm trying to catch something on the scanner about a babysitter and the baby's stopped breathing but there's an ease, a sureness in his stranger's voice that stops me still. It's as if he *knows* me.

'Hey Fin, I heard you're coming to the ice with us. I'm ringing to fill you in on a couple of things. I've been nominated by some of the blokes.'

He tells me our ship's to be the first into the ice after winter, the only ship to crack its way so far south so soon into the season in mid-September. No-one else is as mad as the Aussies. He says we'll be carrying nine tonnes of freeze-dried food on board just in case the ship gets bogged. It's happened before. The baby's being taken to hospital. And the babysitter.

'A journalist, eh?'

'Yeah, a journalist.'

'You know, there's a bit of a rule among us old timers. It's called Blame the Journo. If anything goes wrong, we blame the journo. Just thought I better let you know.'

He chuckles. I swallow his chuckle in mine.

'One last thing. Are you married? A couple of the blokes wanted me to ask. They've heard you on the radio.'

I tell him I'm not married. I hang up, smiling.

Sarey my mate tosses it in, walks out two minutes before the 8 a.m. flagship bulletin. She's never going near the newsroom again. Says she's going to get a life. Won't even come back to fill out release forms. She wants a postcard from Antarctica. Lots of ice.

'A JAFO, people will call you.'

Ben Linton, four days before departure. He works at the Australian Broadcasting Corporation. He's been to Antarctica three times before and says he has ice in his veins and he can't dig it out. He gives me an Antarctic briefing from a journo's perspective. He's bearded. His hair is ice-white. He stares at my miniskirt. At my pink jacket made out of an old chenille bedspread. It's meant to be ironic. I can tell he doesn't get it.

'Here comes another bloody JAFO they'll say, and no-one'll tell you what it means.'

'What is it?'

'Just Another Fucking Observer.'

'Oh, great.'

I look at the radio newsroom buzzing around us, the rows of computer terminals, the video monitors, the police scanners, the journalists working the phones.

'Do they really hate us that much, Ben?'

He considers. A smile cracks his stern face into a boy's.

'Yeah, they do.'

Lovely. I'm the only journo on this expedition.

Ben strides away past the row of ageing subeditors, intent and turtled at their computer screens, and throws back at me, over a line of concentrating heads, 'Everyone who goes down there comes back a different person. It changes your life.'

'Mate, I'll see if you recognise me at the other end,' I yell back.

The scanner's clogged with shit. A kid's told his dad he saw a girl being pushed into a car at Cabramatta Station. A guy's walked into the Albury Hotel with blood on his hands saying he's just stabbed his boyfriend. A bomb scare at a university, on the day of exams. A Domestic. A Domestic. The airwaves crackle and die. My pen lies still. The scanner coughs. Deceased. The pen is snatched. My body leans. Man washed up near Balmoral. Elderly, naked but for underpants around his neck. Story.

Subs don't even use it. Too many bodies lately.

'Just a derro.'

I put my computer to sleep. My body feels thick with tiredness. The train's late. When I get on it, there's a white-bread sandwich squashed into the corner of the seat. I walk from the station up a back alley to my Kings Cross flat. Outside my building I sidestep a delirium of pigeons as they peck at the orange vomit in the gutter. Last week a woman in a short skirt walked up the alley ahead of me with blood in dried ribbons down the inside of her legs. It looked like river lines on a map.

I step into the quiet of my foyer, check the empty mailbox, ride the lift to the fifth floor and open the door and stride through the apartment and fling wide the protesting windows to let in the sky. And stop. My arms are folded on the sill and I lean my face outside and stare at the busy blue before me, the high buildings pushing up into it and the steady march of the aeroplanes traversing it. High above the blue is a clot of cloud and I stretch my face to it and think about those who experience versus those who observe and wonder how Antarctica could change me.

A drink'd be nice. I've started to drink a lot lately. By myself. In my room. I feel like I'm entering a cliche. I make myself a gin and tonic. It doesn't hit the spot. I think about my flatmate. Our living arrangement has soured. His smell has soaked into the walls of my apartment like the cold does in winter. He's accidentally gassed me twice with the oven and he leaves the toilet seat up and he's in the army reserve and he says negative instead of no and out instead of goodbye. I used to think he was cute until he started sleeping with a schoolmate I invited over for coffee. I haven't quite made up my mind to kick him out. Who else would I find? It takes a certain type to want to live in this area.

My apartment building's called The Hopes. What joker thought that one up? I pour myself another drink.

Why do I sleep with my eyes wide open? My Magritte dream: I'm sitting at my desk by the police scanner, forehead furrowed, sunrise behind me through the window which I never see, story story, scanner ticking. And then the 3.25 alarm. Awake, rise, work. Exactly as the dream.

Kings Cross. 3.45 a.m. Venus Club glowing, Tender Trap thumping. Eyes at me as I walk quick along the drag, incongruous in office clothes. Fear. A cabbie's weariness as I squelch onto the plastic over the front passenger seat.

'Jeez, you smell fresh. Just out of a shower, huh? Just washed your hair? You smell soo beautiful. Off to work luv, at this hour?'

I tell him I'm a radio reporter.

'A reporter? Aren't you a good little worker.

There's a big smash along Parramatta Road for you. Looks like a double fatal. They wouldn't let me stop and look.'

I give him a big tip, on the cab docket, at the company's expense.

'Jeez it's good to smell you,' he says as I step from the car.

The phone rings early. It's Jim.

'I just wanted to say hello again, fill you in a little bit more.'

It's the voice of a plumber or a mechanic or a man with a shed. There's a sweetness in it. I'm not used to those sort of voices in my job.

'There's gonna be a hundred and two people on the ship. About twenty-four crew and then the rest are expeditioners. That's what we're called. Pretty grand, eh? And then among the expeditioners you've got scientists and tradesmen— boffins and tradies. That's the lingo.'

I ask him where JAFOs fit into the picture.

'Jafos? Aren't they what you roll down the aisles?'

He tells me his name in Antarctica is Stiff. I don't believe him. He says it's true. He won't tell me how he got it. How could I keep a straight face when I'm calling a man Stiff? I tell him I'll be calling him Jim. I get the feeling that people turn into something else when they're down there, and a new name's just the start of it.

He asks if I mind him ringing up all the time, but it's because he always thinks of new things to tell me. I tell him I don't mind and he says good because he likes ringing me up.

I hang up, smiling again.

Family killed on the north coast. Six bodies, the mother and her five kids, all dead, all in the station wagon. Good story—kids are good, they use kids. On a holiday from the Territory. All in the station wagon. Five kids. Story story.

What has happened to me? A mother and five kids are dead and the strongest reaction I've got is the sweet hit of exhilaration that my story, my voice report, is leading the midday bulletin.

Home. Approaching delirium tiredness. I lie on my bed in the hot afternoon. Sleep is sparse, cobwebbed, in thin strands. There are drills and shouts and bottle recycling trucks and sirens and footsteps and music loud around me.

•

The next day. Jolted out of a quiet news day stupor by a voice from the scanner. A voice taut, bottled up with something huge, a voice to be snapped.

CONSTABLES DOWN SHOT and it's garbled and the voice can't get it clearly out. The man in the police radio control room is infuriating in his calmness.

'Slow down, constable . . . what are you saying . . . we can't understand you.'

SHOT POLICE MATES DOWN DOWN AWAY TWO.

Police down! Police hit! The chill of it. And with the radio control man there's a sudden snap and panic reaching out across the airwaves to all the police officers listening in their squad cars and at their stations and to all the journos straining at the desks in their newsrooms: 'Can *anyone* understand what he's saying?'

And gradually the young policeman's breathing normalises, his mind unjumbles, the story unfolds as he drives to the hospital with a mate dying on the seat beside him and a mate dying on the seat behind him and it's action stations, all systems alert.

It's only much later, much later, leaving work and walking through the park that I crumple and start shaking and have to sit on a park bench for a very long time. I feel wound up as tight as a tin toy. I want to cry with it all but I can't.

I'm being sent to Antarctica to capture noises. The people and the penguins and the machines and the ice and the sounds I don't know about yet.

I pack a hotwater bottle for my tape recorder, to keep it warm in its esky. I pack coolpaks of beautiful, bubbled, marine-blue liquid that will turn into heatpaks when I soak them in hot water. They're for my esky too. I pack lots of batteries because the cold will leech them quickly of power. I pack splicing tape and razor blades and computer disks; I pack a labyrinth of microphone leads and crisp, fresh notepads. I pack condoms. I pack three tubs of moisturiser because my old World Book tells me that Antarctica's the driest continent on earth.

I feel like an eighteenth century explorer as I carefully fill my trunks. I run out of room. I ditch the farewell teddy bear Lyn and the newsroom's given me. I ditch the box of condoms—they're too presumptuous, anyway.

I'm still packing at three on the morning I

depart for Hobart to catch the boat. The plane from Sydney leaves at six-thirty, I haven't yet slept, there's no time. In the weeks before departure my mind's been crammed with busyness, there are lists and purchases and bills, requests and research and farewells. I haven't stopped.

'You're always running,' my father says to me earlier that evening when he phones farewell and I can't talk for long because another farewell dinner's already begun.

'You're never doing nothing, are you, darling?'

'No, I guess not.'

I think back to the galloping days of preparation. I can't remember them too well.

My father pauses over the line.

'Have you seen the full moon? It's a beauty tonight.'

His voice is soaked in stillness. He's ringing from his house by the lake three hours south by car. I haven't seen the moon. I never do; it never reaches into my city. I live in the most populated square-kilometre in Australia. It's a suburb of bedsits in tall buildings and half loaves of bread in the delis.

The Antarctic Division's sent several booklets in the mail. One's called *Separation*. It's about coping with being isolated from your partner. It talks, with great care, about how to make the situation work. It doesn't apply to me. The last bloke I slept with used to hold onto my hair as the alarm went off for work. My head would snap back as I willed myself out of bed and sleep. The last bloke I slept with used to ask, all the time, why I was always so tired. The last bloke was eleven months ago.

I've made the taxi driver's day. As we drive to Sydney airport his enthusiasm makes me feel famous. There's something innocent about it that pushes a smile through my tiredness.

'Wow, Antarctica, wow.'

The taxi driver thumps the wheel. I won't be surprised if he starts radioing all his taxi mates in his excitement.

'You know I read in the *Reader's Digest* that this bloke down there ate two pounds of butter a day because of its fat. It's so cold down there it burns all the fat.'

'Really?'

'Yep. My wife lived in Alaska for two years. She never felt better or happier.'

There's no irony in his voice.

'You know, if there's a car broken down on the side of the road up there and you drive past it without stopping, and the person dies, you can be charged with murder.' He thumps the wheel again. 'Are you really going to the South Pole or are you joking?'

'No, not the South Pole. Antarctica, the continent. Not the spot in the middle of it.'

'Oh Antarctica, South Pole—same thing. Don't you have to get your appendix out for that?'

'Um, I don't know.'

'Well you'll have to find out pretty quick.' He pulls up at the airport terminal. 'Say hello to the polar bears for me. Is it all ice or is there land under there somewhere?'

I tell him there are no polar bears and it's not just ice. And there are no Eskimos. I tip him well. He tells me to make sure I stop if I see someone pulled up on the side of the road. I tell him I don't think there are any roads down in Antarctica. He says oh.

My mother's with me on the plane to Hobart. She's flying down from Sydney to see me off at the dock. She wants to know, relentlessly and annoyingly, details about Pat Pisano. Is he married yet? How many children does he have? Did his mother remarry? Did his father? Are they still in the same street? I answer shortly and swiftly. I tell her he stuck his finger up my bum. She's intrigued. She says she's never had anything up her bottom in her life. I remind her about the suppositories for her migraines. She says oh yes, those.

In careful paper she gives me a gift of ginger tablets and a box of ginger tea.

'It's good for seasickness, darling. Try it.'

I smile. No-one but my mum would give me such a farewell present.

Mid-December, five years earlier. The QEII on an Atlantic crossing, Southampton to New York. A six-day voyage. I vomit twenty-one times. The situation feels unendurable, yet it has to be endured. There's no way out of it, no way to remove myself from the bellowing roll of the ship because even if I was magnificently wealthy, a hired helicopter would never reach that far. On day five I hold my forehead tightly and go down the stairs to the surgery to join the queue to get a needle in my bottom. The sharp, tart stench of other people's vomit crowds thickly at me as I descend. I feel like I'm climbing down into a Breughel painting. On the deck of the surgery the crew's changing the carpet in the corridor, because it's been splashed with the vomit of so many people. The carpet, me, the cabin, we're all branded by smell.

'I am never, ever going on a sea voyage again,' I declare to my mother, at the airport, on my return. I mean it.

And now, Antarctica. To get to it I have to cross the Great Southern Ocean. My World Book tells me it's the roughest ocean in the world.

'It's the chance of a lifetime, isn't it? I have to go. I can't not. I can't say no, can I?'

The land of mythical tragedies. The place of ships' hulls being crushed by ice, of long treks into darkness and death, of soles falling from feet and being strapped back on, of teeth freezing and splitting, fingers dying, toenails coming away, mates disappearing through holes in the ice, mates walking away into blizzards, saying I'm just going outside and may be some time, and never coming back, of men lying down to die and placing their hand across the chest of their already dead, dear mate.

It's the most isolated place on earth. The coldest and the windiest. The lowest temperature ever recorded is −89.6°C. The highest wind speed, 320 kilometres an hour.

Lyn's exact words when she found out it was me who'd been given the Antarctica assignment were, Bitch bitch pig bitch. Her envy was magnificent. Who could refuse the offer after envy like that? An offer that gets me off the early shift and out of the newsroom and away from Kings Cross for a while.

Who could refuse?

TWO

BELLY RINGS

AND BEARDS

I always feel as if my blood thickens when I come to Tasmania, from cold or something. I sense within me a kind of slowing and I tell myself it's not such a bad thing.

The sky hangs low. It touches the Hobart rooftops. From the dark closeness of the rain-soaked city we'll be sailing south into a dazzling world of long white light. We'll be leaving behind raincoats and umbrellas and taking special filters for our cameras and skin and eyes.

The taxi climbs through the mist to the head-quarters of the Australian Antarctic Division. The complex is high on the edge of the city. The taxi passes a convoy of trucks winding slowly down the mountain. On the trucks' flat backs are tree trunks piled high and shaved ragged like giant shaggy pencils. The taxi driver lifts his finger from the wheel in a salute to the truckies and in his small movement there's pride at those trucks.

'Why on earth would you want to go to Antarctica, eh? It's too bloody cold for me. I've never been out of Tassie. Everything I need is here.'

The taxi driver talks affably and slowly. He hands across his crudely printed business card at the end of the ride. He wants the fare to the airport, on my way out of town several months down the track. I tell him I'll put his card somewhere safe.

'You do that.'

Antarctica is arse end up on the display globe that rests on a pedestal in the Division's bright head-quarters of steel and glass and white. Stout Tasmanians walk the wide aisles. There are heavy mountain boots and knobbly jumpers. There's shy-ness in scrubbed faces. There are many beards. Jim's among it all somewhere. There's curiosity at my layers of inner-city black. I'm here to be kitted out.

I'm wearing too much makeup and I'm walk-ing too fast.

Cec's domain is a long room in the bowels of

the Division. He's tall at the counter and fast disappearing behind his stomach. Behind him stretch racks of clothes and shelves of boots and hats. He fingers the Antarctic clothes with a longing to be there.

He dumps in front of me men's thermal long johns with a slice at the front for the penis. Then huge sheepskin lined boots that encase my toes in a close roof of steel. Then woollen trousers and shirts and a jumper. They're all bloke-sized. The only things that look like they'll fit are very black eye protectors called glacier goggles.

'I'll give you a tip. Make sure you put sun-cream underneath your nose and your eyebrows and your ears. Everyone forgets about the reflection from the ground, it's a real killer.'

Then Cec leans close. He drops his voice. He tells me he knows the people who'll be difficult 'down south'.

'They're a bloody pain to kit out. They're fussy and demanding and take forever. I ring upstairs to the voyage leaders and warn them. I've never been wrong. There's one guy to watch out for—'

A man comes up to the counter.

Cec switches his tone. 'Layers are the key. If

you wear lots of clothes you create pockets of warm air and you're insulated. If you only wear one big thing you can sweat in that and the sweat freezes and then you get frostbite.'

'You're kidding.'

'True. Some of Scott's party sweated so much that their clothes froze as stiff as boards. The men got stuck in a stooping position when they were pulling their sledges, so they couldn't stand up straight. Imagine that.' I don't need to. Cec is demonstrating. 'It was a bloody nightmare. And *then* they got frostbite. It was just incredible. Their fingers were covered in blisters, and the liquid in them froze, and their hands came up like bunches of frozen grapes.'

He dumps in front of me a huge yellow jumpsuit with padded silk lining.

I climb into it. I feel like I'm stepping into an elaborate costume for a pantomime. It's called a freezer suit and it's busy all over with pockets and zips. Its smell is a rich cocktail of a man who's sweated too much and a man's unwashed groin.

Cec gets it back.

'Phew! That goes into the incinerator.' He tosses the jumpsuit into a corner. Its legs and arms splay like a fallen scarecrow.

Another suit's dumped in front of me. I smell it. Clean. The crotch comes down to my knees and the arms extend fifteen centimetres beyond my fingertips. The name HONEST JOHN is bold in fat texta across my left breast.

'Done,' says Cec, contemplating and nodding and chuckling in matey approval with the man in line next to me.

'If only Honest John could see his freezer suit now.'

I suspect I look like the Michelin Man. Or a penguin. 'Are you laughing at me, Cec? Is this because I'm a journo?'

I'm joking but he leans forward and rests his elbows on the counter, officialdom shutting down his face. He says he's not laughing at me. He says he's the sexual harassment officer for the Antarctic Division and there've been problems down south in the past.

'Young girls who are just out of uni, and they end up having sleepless nights. Women haven't been going down for that long, you know. There was a lot of resistance from the blokes at first. If anything happens, tell people. And for God's sake, you girls give each other support.'

I thank him and ram all my gear down tight

into a cylindrical canvas pack. My kitbag is weighted with boots and bloke-sized items of clothing. I hump it onto my shoulder like a swagman.

'Do you need any help with that, kid? It's almost as big as you are!'

'I can handle it.'

I sway, smile and collect my legs for the walk out the door. Halfway up the corridor I remember I forgot to ask who was the guy to watch out for. I'm not humping the bloody pack back. I'll have to find out for myself.

A crowded auditorium. A briefing by the Antarctic Division's legal department. Jim's in here somewhere. I try to match a face to his voice. There are too many beards. I give up. People stare at my clothes, the urban black. Some cock their heads to the person sitting next to them. That must be that journalist, I imagine they're saying. The one and only JAFO on the voyage and I feel like I'm standing out like tits on a bull. I have to win these people's trust. I don't feel I belong. I'm the only one in the auditorium who hasn't had field training and who didn't have to sit the five hundred question British army psychology test. I'm thinking about missing the Sleaze Ball in Sydney and my belly ring, which my skin's in the process of rejecting, and whether I should've had my appendix removed.

A line of suits walks to the seats on the podium. There's a hush from the new expeditioners. A man comes in late and sits in the empty seat next to me. The lights dim. A list of rules comes up brightly on an overhead projector. A woman from the Division's legal department stands with a long pointer stick and explains. Her nervousness contradicts the crispness of her suit. I write down in my notepad what she says. Work, for me, has begun. The man who's late places his arm on the rest beside me. The veins run close under the skin. They stand out like thick cords. I can't help staring at them.

'You can't take rocks from the continent because if everyone took them, there'd be a problem.'

He's wearing a green woollen jumper and it's scrunched up above his elbows. It has a hole in it.

'You can't take polystyrene balls to the continent, because they don't degrade and they get stuck in the throats of animals and birds and choke them.'

His wrist flops over the edge of the armrest. I think about Michelangelo wrists and how immensely erotic I find them. I imagine his hipbone. I find hipbones immensely erotic too. And feet. And throats.

The legal woman finds her stride and the tremor in her voice disappears. I focus on my notepad.

'Now the big one.' She smiles apologetically. 'You can't consume more than three cans of beer a day on the ship. It's a safety issue. Last year someone got drunk and got their foot stuck in an automatically closing watertight door, and the foot was almost severed. If the three-can rule doesn't work on this voyage, the next one'll be dry. You lot won't be very popular if you blow it for the voyages behind you. Think about it.'

It'll be a good excuse to kick this drinking habit which I'm starting to like too much. I don't drink beer anyway. The man bends over to tie up a shoelace on his walking boot. He smells, softly, of a wet garden. He smells of sweat. Not clammy, ugly, office polystyrene-shirt sweat. Sweat from working and walking outdoors.

'And lastly, don't leave anything of your presence in the field.'

He stops tying his laces.

'Except footprints. Cigarette butts and faeces and everything human in terms of waste is to be removed, because it will never, *ever* rot.'

He sits up.

'Urinating *is* allowed, but preferably down a crack in the ice.'

'How good's your aim?' he turns and says quietly to me. We laugh. The noise punches into the talk. Heads turn. I feel like a schoolgirl at the back of the class. His voice isn't Jim's. When the lecture's over I smile in farewell and he smiles back and I get out of the room quickly. I'm scared that if I say anything, I'll spoil it all.

'It's an urban myth,' says the doctor ahead of me in the cafeteria line. 'Your appendix is perfectly safe. The only people who have to have them removed are us doctors. And that's because a Russian doctor got appendicitis in the early sixties and had to operate on himself. He used a local anaesthetic, a scalpel and a mirror. And the chef as an assistant. The appendix is still at a Russian station, in a jar, on display, as a warning to the rest of us.'

I imagine it, vividly, as I wait for my banana

sandwich. Imagine slicing into my belly with a scalpel, the uprush of blood, lifting the inflamed appendix out, sewing up my own skin, the small tents of flesh as the thread drags through it. I'm not very good with blood.

'You've got nothing to worry about,' says the doctor, smiling, into my thoughts. 'No-one dies in Antarctica anymore.'

He can't help with the belly ring. He says to take it out.

The night before departure the pub across from the dock is dense with noise and smoke and smells of beer and sweat. It's a pre-sailing Antarctic tradition and there are expeditioners and partners and parents and mates. Hans, a Division official, introduces me to tight groups of people. They check out the clothes. From the women there's shyness and reticence and suspicion, and from the men, curiosity. Hans drifts away. I look for the man who sat next to me in the auditorium. I can't see him and I'm relieved.

I wander, get another drink, catch conversation scraps. A man tells two others, 'Mate, she fucks like a vomiting dog.' They stop and stare as

I pass. I go to the toilet. I look at myself in the mirror. The lights are blue so people can't find their veins for needles. Hobart surprises me. I'm definitely wearing too much makeup. I scrub away my browned city-lips. My belly ring's hurting. I flip up my shirt. The skin around my navel's red and puffy. I push the ring out. I'll leave it with Mum for when I get back.

As I come from the bathroom I pass the trio again. 'I told her, you're beautiful, but you'd be more beautiful with my balls on your chin.' There's long, loud laughter. I wonder what I'm getting myself into. I think of my bloke-sized freezer suit. The way it masks my body shape. You wouldn't even know I was a girl in it, with the balaclava and goggles on. I'll have to unzip the suit to piss on the ice. The man from the auditorium will have to unzip his suit to piss on the ice. God knows what's ahead. I don't stay long at the pub. I'm not very good in crowds.

My brother Simon rings the Hobart hotel room, late, to say farewell. I tell him about the pub and he chuckles and he says I'll be lucky to get ten minutes to myself on the boat. I'm fierce with my solitude and Simon knows it. He is too. He says with glee in his voice to keep him informed, as if he knows it's going to be a disaster right from the start. He tells me he wants the spew count. He tells me he asked Mum why she was travelling all the way to Hobart with me just to say goodbye.

'Because you might never come back,' she said, and she was laughing. She said remember Perth, and then Alice Springs, how you say you're only going to be away for a little while and then you don't come back for a very long time.'

Simon laughs and then stops. 'You *are* going to come back, aren't you?'

'You'll have to wait and see.'

'If you don't come back, Finny, can I have your car?'

Twenty-odd years ago Simon gave me the name Fin. It was somewhere in the thick of a childhood summer, when I was always running away to the baths on the edge of the surf on the edge of the day. I would slice through the thick water and yell to my brother, 'Five minutes, five minutes' as he stood on the edge of the pool and shouted at me to come for tea. And one day walking home he called me 'you old fin' as he flicked me with a towel and I ran away, and the name for his fish of a sister was picked up by others and it spread and it stuck. I held it beyond the splintering of my family into adulthood, like a teddy bear from a childhood that's been kept by a pillow for years. It's the only thing, besides photographs, that I've kept from that time. Oh, and a hole in my ear. When I was nine Simon pierced my earlobe using a needle and a potato and a banana paddlepop to numb the pain. The paddlepop didn't work. It hurt so much I wouldn't let him do the other one. I'm not good with pain.

What I don't tell Simon as I say goodbye from my high Hobart hotel room, is that one of the reasons I'm always running away and not coming back for a very long time is that I can't be in the same city as my mother for too long. It creates enormous problems. Her standards are too high and I feel like I can never quite please her and it's all so much easier at a distance. She's fond of telling me I've got a lot of growing up to do. I prefer to do it away from her gaze.

That night I say goodnight to her as she reads English *Vogue* in the wide hotel bed beside me. We haven't touched for a long time. I lean across and kiss her, my lips to a cheek that's soaked in Elizabeth Arden moisturiser. It's a smell that plunges me

back to my childhood. I wonder what Antarctica
will smell like. My mother looks surprised at my
sudden fierce affection and she asks me why I'm
kissing her.

'I don't know.'

'You're a funny thing,' she says, serious, contemplating. She holds my chin and looks at my
face. I have two pimples on my chin and the
beginning of my first wrinkle between my eyebrows. I shouldn't be getting pimples anymore. I
move my face away from her gaze. I feel like a dog
being inspected. My mother laughs. 'I've always
thought you were a funny thing.'

Tomorrow, the ship sails.

THREE

SHIP AWAY

There are two six-foot-long couches. They're face to face, with a slim space between them. I lift the base of one and it flips, reluctantly, into a bunk. Another bunk's strapped flat against the wall. Processed air hums. The walls are close.

It's home for the next five weeks.

A neat line of matching luggage already claims one of the couches. My gaggle of boxes and backpacks and trunks and shopping bags is dumped on the other couch. I'm sharing with two other women I know nothing about.

The bathroom's like a spaceship capsule. Everything's small and plastic. I go to the toilet, then afterwards, when I depress the lever, nothing happens. I depress it again. I've done one very large shit and it's not going anywhere. I can see bits of my dinner from last night in it.

Bad, bad start.

I knock on the cabin next door and hope I'll be back before either bunkmate wants to use the bathroom. The door of the adjoining cabin's ajar. I see an arm with thick veins reaching up to put a Scotch bottle on a shelf. It's him. Oh no. The door opens.

It's not him.

'What?' No friendliness or curiosity or welcome in the voice.

I tell him my toilet isn't working and he says none are and the engineers are trying to fix the problem and that at this very moment they're wading waist-deep in the sewerage tank and a message came over the intercom fifteen minutes ago. I was on deck.

I tell him I'm the journalist and he says uh huh. I tell my name and he says I know. He doesn't tell me his.

I go back to my cabin. Bad start.

Andrea Everitt extends her hand. She shaves her chin. There's a peppering of black hairs, their blunt beginnings. Maybe she's into steroids. Andrea's from Wollongong. She's lean and toned and pretty and she'll be sleeping a metre above me for the next six weeks.

We unpack. We find the lightswitch and turn it on because the mean salt-scoured porthole doesn't let in much daylight. Andrea tells me she's a glaciologist. She describes herself as obsessed by ice. She's going to Antarctica to help measure the largest glacier in the world.

'It's the most incredible feeling, to put your bare hand on an iceberg, to touch its stillness.'

My mother's given me a farewell block of chocolate. I share it and we laugh—Andrea says she's obsessed by chocolate too. We'll get on well. She says she's got some chocolate in her bags, a packet of Smarties, and I keep on unpacking as she finds the packet and sits down and opens it and eats the lot by herself. I've finished unpacking. I sit on my couch and read the ship safety flyer to get my mind off the Smarties. Andrea puts on her jacket and without a word strides out the door and flicks off the light.

The air hums. The light's tepid. It's like a blanket's been thrown over me.

The corridors are thin. I flatten myself against walls

to let past people who are burdened with backpacks and boxes. Men smells press close. There are shy hellos and polite stepping backs, 'You go', 'No you', and smiles. The man from the auditorium isn't anywhere to be seen. I've been thinking a lot about his wrists. A small staircase leads to the green metal sweep of the helicopter deck. It's high and spare at the rear of the ship. Two shiny choppers are in the opened-up hangar. Their ends are outside like bees in the holes of a hive. My body's buoyed by the creak bounce of the mesh in the tall fence that cages the helideck. Harbour water's inky and oily and dark beneath me and the sky's blue and wide and I'm alone and it's sweet.

'Chippie to Jafo, Chippie to Jafo, come in Jafo.'

It's the voice from the telephone. The voice comes booming and muffled from a piece of cardboard rolled into a megaphone.

'Jim! Put that down!' I'm laughing. 'I thought you told me Jafos are something you roll down the aisle.'

'Maybe they are.'

A surfer's smile. Lines that cut deep around his eyes. A young face. A body that looks as if it's been slapped by sun and salt since he was a toddler. I remember now. Born in Coolangatta.

'You know what a chippie is, Miss Lois?'

''Course I do. A chippie's a carpenter.'

'Too right. We'll get on well.'

'Hey Jimbo, give us a hand, mate!' The yell soars across to us from someone burdened on the other side of the helideck.

'If you need any questions answered, come and seek me out. Cabin D21, or the bar. It's my office!'

And he's gone. I smile. Hold the prospect of him like a slow chocolate in my mouth. He's an ordinary bloke. Dad would approve. He wishes upon his children nothing but ordinary lives. He's got two new kids. I asked him at my farewell barbecue what he hoped the new lot would be and he said to me, quietly, they're only average kids, they'll get a trade, nothing flash. There was relief in his voice as he said it and he'd turned and looked, bewildered, at me. My father's a builder. He can't understand why I want to go to Antarctica. It's not the sort of thing a young woman should be doing. I know he won't be listening to my reports that'll be beamed back to the mainland by satellite. He doesn't listen to my radio station. He says the voices are too posh.

My mother, on the other hand, is always wrangling with the bloody-minded tenacity of mediocrity. She wishes for her children lives and things that aren't ordinary. She wishes for them everything that she didn't have growing up in her fishing town. With her daughter, the campaign began with the sound of her voice. Elocution lessons from the age of five. It's no wonder my parents split. As Raymond Carver says, their energy was all wrong.

I fall back against the mesh of the fence and watch the tight knots of families and lovers and friends. I watch the engineers who are protective around the expensive complexity of the helicopters. Their eyes are on a line of snotty looking kids stretching shy grubby hands to a machine's shiny belly, as if they're patting the side of a very quiet horse.

The mess is crammed. The captain, Tony Crane, addresses us. He wears a baseball cap. He tells us we're going on the last great sea voyage in the world—to the wild side of Antarctica where no plane can land, across the roughest ocean in the world. There are groans. He calls for a volunteer to demonstrate an immersion suit. There's a reluctant hush.

'Get the journo.' The yell from the back of the room is Jim's.

'Thanks, Stiff. Mate.'

I step forward, willing myself not to blush. The suit's of thick rubber, like a giant baggy wetsuit. Captain Crane says it's in case the ship starts sinking, when there's the likelihood of us ending up in Antarctic waters that have an average temperature of −1.8°C. The suit has built-in feet. I have to sit on the floor to get into it. Bands of severe rubber clamp tightly around my wrists. It's hard to poke my hands through. I'm taking a long time. People are laughing. I'm blushing. My fingers are getting panicky and annoyed. I finally stand and the captain pulls the hood over my head and pulls a flap tightly across my nose and mouth. I'm gagged by rubber. All that's exposed is a sliver of eyes.

'This is the way we like our journos,' Captain Crane says.

There's laughter from the mess. When I pull away the suit there's a round of applause.

We're herded on deck for the next instalment. The lifeboats.

A fibreglass orange bubble that floats. Inside, it glows yellow, like a church, from the sun through the fibreglass. Strange shoulders and thighs press close. The man from the auditorium climbs in late, last. Without looking, he sits opposite me. He's had a haircut. His greyness is cropped close, he's almost bald. He looks across and catches my eye. He beams. He points to his head and pulls a stricken face. I smile. I can't tell his age. He could be ten years older than me, or twenty. I like older men. They teach me things.

We're in a lifeboat that seats seventy. It's completely enclosed, like a mini submarine that floats. We've been crank-jerked over the side of the ship for a chug around Hobart Harbour. There's laughter as three mobile phones intrude into the safety talk. Feet thud and scrape on the fibreglass. Diesel fumes thread through the air.

'Thank God there isn't a swell.'

Someone from the rear, loudly.

'I've been in one of these in Bass Strait, and a bag of vomit was passed from person to person, and there was vomit on vomit.'

The sparse chatter stops.

'No-one was spared. Even if they didn't feel

like having a go at first, they did when the bag got to them.'

The stiffness among strangers is snapped. There's a collapse of groans and exclamations and laughter.

The man and I smile wryly at each other. The man next to him catches us out. He stares at me.

Paper streamers arc in slow spirals as they plummet from the high decks of the ship to the concrete of the dock. The streamers are in faded, fusty fifties pastels, as if they've absorbed sun and dust in a corner-shop window for a very long time. Bags of tight coils are passed from expeditioner to expeditioner like gifts. The coils are missiled strongly into the throng of faces and hands beneath them, are picked up and caught by children and adults and even a blue cattledog tries to get in on the act, its jaws snapping at paper and missing until it's tangled and twisting and is firmly pulled still by a woman at its collar and there's laughter and shouting and whistling and waving, cameras and video cameras and a local television crew and then high over it all, the ship's magisterial horn.

There's a hush. The ship comes gently from the dock. The streamers tense and softly snap. The ship is away.

I quickly lose the vivid black and camel smartness of my mother in the crowd. The man's suddenly beside me. I feel tight in the chest. I tell myself to be cool.

'She's mine . . . the dog.'

She's standing on the very edge of the dock, panting and barking and whining at our receding ship. The man extends a still and strong arm to her in farewell.

'Spani, she's called. After spanakopita. It's one of my favourite dishes.'

'Well I hope you also like frozen vegetables, because I suspect we've got a lot of them ahead.'

The answer's not great but it's okay and he tells me his name is Max and he's a biologist from Melbourne. He's worked with penguins on Macquarie Island and possums in northern Victoria and he's now in management, tied to a desk. He says he pushed for a chance to get his hands dirty again. He grabbed the Antarctic project when it was offered. He's going to be studying crabeater seals, which live entirely on the ice floating around Antarctica. He says the seals are extremely elusive and difficult to catch. He wants to know a lot about me. He asks what I want to get out of the trip and I say I'm not sure, I don't really know what's ahead. He says it's been his dream to get to Antarctica since he was a cub scout. I tell him all I know about scouts is that the local scoutmaster got my brother to deal drugs for him when he was eleven and we're laughing as the man who was next to Max in the lifeboat comes up to us and tells Max that he'd better go downstairs and put his seasickness patch on and Max says yeah. He introduces his friend. Jack. I shake Jack's hand and the touch is light, like a whisper. Max's eyes smile at me and the men are gone.

I didn't tell Max that something I want from the trip is uncomplicated air. It's difficult to explain. I want to settle into my skin, reclaim it with rest and removal from my crammed city existence. I feel as if the city's frantic energy has soaked through me, I feel as if my job is consuming my life.

Breeze comes at me. Hobart shrinks.

'She's great in the ice, but she bobs like a cork in the open water.'

Jim, as we sail up the ribbon of river to the ocean beyond. He's on deck with two cups of coffee. He hands one to me. I don't drink coffee. Politeness forces sparrow sips as Jim explains with the concentration of a boy with a new model boat just why it is that our ship bobs around like a cork. The hull's shaped like a spoon. Other ships have hulls with spines that taper to a point. The belly on ours is flattened so it can ride up on top of the huge slabs of ice in its path and crack them with its weight.

'And sometimes we get bogged.'

He grins.

'The great thing about getting bogged is that the ship's still, not like what's ahead of us in the Southern Ocean. Fin, they don't call them the Roaring Forties for nothing.'

A headache's seeping into the front of my forehead and I'm not sure if it's the coffee or the cram of the final packing or the ship's sudden rocking. The hull pushes strongly to the river heads. There's an optimistic rhythm to the ship's quickening, like a horse that's straining at the reins at the smell of home.

Jim's left on deck holding the bleak remains of a cold cup of coffee. I go downstairs and brush

by the man from the cabin next door in a thin
corridor and he clicks his tongue, exasperated. It's
as though he's surrounded himself with a boundary
of no. He makes me feel wrong. In my cabin I take
the ginger tablets, stick the seasickness patch firmly
behind my ear and lie on the bunk, not looking
from the porthole, not seeing the end of land and
not caring that I'm not seeing it.

The thick smell of cigarettes hovers around Blanca
Garcia's skin and breath. There's less than a metre
between us at night. Her loose and large body is
undecided, asleep and awake and asleep and awake,
loudly, in the bunk opposite me.

'I do not know about this cold I am going
into. I am from the sun.'

Blanca Garcia is from Spain. She's on a scientific exchange program and she's the only foreigner
on the voyage. She roams the ship restlessly by day
and long into the night.

'I am not good with ships.'

She studies phytoplankton from the waters of
the Southern Ocean. Her micro-organisms jiggle in
Petri dishes in a lab in the bowels of the ship. She
calls her micro-organisms her babies and she has

three complaints. The rumble of the ship's engine that's sickening her babies, the three beers a day policy, and the lack of fuckable men.

'These Australian men are not like Spanish men. These Aussies are, what you say, docile. We are a cabin of three single women. It is a ship of men. There is something wrong.'

'Maybe we're not working hard enough, Blanca.'

A grin lights her face.

'Yah, darling. Maybe.'

'Hey, give it time,' yells Andrea from the bathroom.

I sit in Jim's office in a dark corner of the bar and he tells me how he used to be a cleaner until one day he started scrubbing away at his shadow on the wall and he realised then it was time to quit. Jim says they called him Clean Shadow in Antarctica, until his last trip, when they changed it to Stiff.

'It's much better,' he says, but still won't explain how he got it.

Jim's in the bar a lot. At the fag end of night I see him with wet eyes and sodden skin. I suspect he's one of those men that can only ever approach a woman about a fuck if he's comfortably drunk. He asks me if he can have my beer allocation. I say sure. He's probably got a stash of spirits in his cabin too. I tell myself I'm not interested. I'm on the wagon and there's a lot of history in Jim's surfer's eyes and it's bleak and sad.

He's lying in a corridor, late, after a video. He's fallen. Jack comes up behind us and steps over Jim without saying a word. I help Jim up. I watch Jack walk away down the corridor. His tallness seems to fill up the corridor. There's a strange stillness about him, in his walk and his talk and the way he wears his neat-fitting jeans. There's a contained, quiet, non-blokey carefulness, a thoroughness. I don't like it. It's cold.

Jim examines his elbow.

'Another bloody bruise, I bet.'

I smile. He asks me what I'm doing for the next fifty years.

Small bruises, like puffs of brown cloud, are appearing in odd places all over my body. The bruises are from floating into walls and table corners and door handles as I walk around in the deepening roll of the ship. It's getting rougher.

Word passes around the corridors. A plumber's been taken to the ship's hospital. He's been put on a drip because he's so seasick he can't keep anything down. He's dehydrating and starving to death.

As we head deep into the Southern Ocean, Helen, the ship's doctor, tells us not to fight the ship's rock and not to lock our knees. Penny, the ship's dishwasher, whispers to me not to drink tea or coffee. Simeon, a mechanical engineer, instructs me to wedge myself into my bunk with pillows. Simeon sits like a toad in the noisy bowels of the ship. He's fleshy and old and so moistly white it's as if his mother's kept him locked away in a very small room since he was a baby. We sit in the rumbling, clanking engine room and he tells me about the ship. He speaks of it like a beautiful fuck. He tells me she's double hulled, with two skins of steel, so she won't be crushed by the ice. He tells me her ribcage is wide and firm and strong and that the reason she's tarted up in a screaming orange colour is so that she can be easily spotted in the vast expanse of ice. He tells me there are several of the crew who have a woman every voyage. He won't tell me who.

The dipping and rolling becomes more savage. The ship's cunningly prepared. I am too. I've got my seasickness patch on and it's working. There are handles on the shower walls to hold onto and chains from the floor of the mess to the underbellies of the chairs, holding them obediently in place. There are flat bands of wood penning books into shelves. The wood's detachable. It's sometimes used as a cricket bat, especially by Patrick, a floppy haired crew member.

'Come and have a hit, Fin.'

'Maybe later. I'm busy working. Tomorrow, huh?'

Patrick's a prospect. He's an officer in his mid-thirties who's jumped across from the navy. I'll keep him on his toes. Flirt, keep him guessing.

Max and Jack wander the ship relentlessly together. They come consistently late to the mess at mealtimes. I'm reluctant to break into the tightness of their companionship. I don't know what's going on between them.

I find out the man in the cabin next to me's called Tyrel. He's the only expeditioner on the ship who's been allocated a cabin to himself. My source can't tell me why. I'll have to dig further. Men, men everywhere.

'Angel gear is a truckie term,' Max says. 'It's when they coast down a hill in neutral. It saves fuel and it's fun but it's highly dangerous. They're not really engaged and they're not doing what they should be doing. And that's sort of how I feel about my life right now. And I guess it's why I leapt at the chance to go to Antarctica.'

We're on the ship's bridge. Horizon is in every direction. Around us are scientists carrying out bird counts and whale watches, there are sextants and depth sounders, binoculars and bustle. We settle into silence in a corner, by a sun-warmed window. I don't feel uncomfortable with the not-talking. We watch an albatross gliding outside. It's keeping soaring pace with the ship.

'You should try and get to Macquarie Island during the resupply, Fin. Do what you can to get on a chopper. It's one of the only islands in the Southern Ocean, and it's crammed with wildlife coming there to breed. The whole island is like a frenzy of hormones.'

We both laugh. Stare at the strong wide albatross. It's the ship's lone pilot to the land.

'The seal population was wiped out late last century by the sealers, and if that wasn't enough, they then decided to get stuck into the penguins.'

His voice is sharp and intelligent and quick and educated. I watch his hand on the glass. There are no rings. The nails are clean and closely cropped.

'I did my penguin survey on the island a decade ago. The numbers are slowly being built back up. If you *do* get there, Fin, watch out for the men. They've turned a bit feral.'

Jack's suddenly behind us. His voice pushes loudly into our small radius.

'Who are you saying is feral?'

Max explains. Jack rolls his eyes and nods in agreement. I turn back to the window to watch the albatross. It's gone. I ask Max if he wants to go out on deck. He does. Jack starts flipping through a whale identification book. The breeze outside is ferocious. I write down bits of what Max has said about Macquarie Island in my notebook and the pages flap and flick in the gusting wind like sheets on a clothesline. Max leans over the railing close to me.

'I can almost smell the island on the breeze now. God, I loved it there.'

Jack comes out and asks us if we want some chocolate. Max says yes. He plunges his hand into Jack's parka pocket and rummages for the block.

I turn and look for the albatross. It's up high and alone, on the other side of the ship. It's hovering, as if it's savouring for a moment its stillness and the wind that's rushing under its wings.

Macquarie's halfway between Tasmania and Antarctica. It's a thin sliver of plunging green in the vastness of the Great Southern Ocean. It supports two mountains that from the ship seem top-heavy for the length of the land. The island's thirty-four kilometres long, three kilometres wide. As we approach, the steep sides of its slopes look gentle in the mist.

'Don't be deceived,' Max says. 'It's a wild old place. The average temperature is four degrees and it doesn't take too kindly to humans.'

We sail closer. The fog concentrates into a thick cloud and drops protectively down over the island, hiding the land from us.

TODD THERE ARE ONLY 3,528 WEETBIX
LEFT, SO WE WORKED IT OUT, ONLY SIX A
DAY.

The words are scrawled loudly on the Macquarie Island mess whiteboard. It's our official greeting.

'Can I start now?'

Todd yells his wide hello to the room. He's a seal biologist returning to the research station at Macca for a twelve-month stint. He's leading the expedition of day-trippers from the ship.

We've come bowed and burdened from beneath the chopper blades. In our arms are boxes of fruit and wine and plump bags of mail. The meat and the lounge chairs and computers and flour bags will come later, in a continuous thump of chopper shuttles.

I dump my box of fruit on the nearest table. The Macca men look like bushrangers. Their beards are full and fierce and long. Max was right. A man called Hump eats four bananas in a row and then says he feels sick. A man called Dog bites ferociously into an apple.

'That's better than sex.'

Then he qualifies it.

'Well, as good as.'

His free hand caresses another apple.

Hump yells across the room, 'Where's the journalist?'

'Here.'

I'm not in the mood for blokey exuberance. I've only got the afternoon and there's no time to get to know the Macquarie Island men and they're not sellable anyway. No producer back home wants an interview with them. They're not on the ice. They're not a sexy enough story. I want to get outside.

'Be careful,' someone yells to me as I zip up my parka in the cold porch, 'or one of us might get you.'

Outside, wet wraps itself around me. There's slick wet wind and rain. It comes every day of the year here. Wind-sheared slopes climb into cloud. Cranky lime-green and white ocean bashes onto beaches of black sand. Surf smashes into jutting rocks and sheer drops of shiny black cliffs. Slimy tendrils of kelp huddle close to the shoreline as if a population of oily-black octopi have come here to die.

I walk along the cliffs. Wind pushes me. I slip. A necklace of shipwrecks rings the island in a grim warning. Some of the wrecks poke up, like ragged shards of glass set into the top of a concrete wall.

Somewhere beyond the shipwrecks, in the thick of the fog, is my ship.

Max has filled me in on the Macca stories. The ship broke its anchor chain on its last trip to the island and drifted dangerously close. Its predecessor sank here. There are ghosts. The ship comes no closer than a kilometre from the shoreline for this trip. The resupply for the fourteen men on the station has to be done entirely by air. The helicopters carry cargo in rope nets slung swinging under their bellies. They thump back and forth. Then they stop.

There's a shout behind me. It's Dog. He comes up to me, panting. The chopper pilots are grounded on the island. They've lost sight of the ship in the dropping down mist and they're not going to risk any flying. The island's my home for the night. Great.

We walk back to the base, winding down from the cliffs through tufts of long yellow grass to the coal-black beaches. Around us are the bark and belch of the elephant seals. They're like giant slugs clumped in close harems on the sand. Strong brown skuas are buffeted by the breeze overhead and the head of a killer whale rises up and then sinks in the furious green of the ocean. Penguins keep an affronted distance, on the beach, and the rocks, and the helipad.

Dog's apologetic and stumbly about the men in the mess. He says the blokiness inside is all bluff and the men have forgotten how to treat women because it's been such a long time. He's sure they'll remember by the time we get back. He coaxes me to put my hand to the coarse black curls of a seal pup, as if to make up for it all.

The fur's stiff and damp and not at all soft. The bull seals peer at us like fat old men peering from behind newspapers in an English club. Some of them break from their stillness with a huff, and lumber away on too-small flippers. They heave-ho their rippling bulk. It's a strange, ugly sort of grace.

Dog tells me the most common thing the doctor treats on the island is seal bites. There's the punch of smell in the wind; it stinks of rotting kelp and salt and wet.

'Gee it's good to see the ship,' Dog says. 'It was so cold this season, the water froze in the pipes. We had to flush the toilets with buckets of sea water. We all got a bit on the nose, but we had a ripper of a year.'

•

His body's softly going to fat. He can hardly touch my breasts. He stares, reaches out, draws back. Then he places a large, cold hand on my chest. The hand stays there for a long time. He's grave and quiet.

The woman I was meant to be sharing the hut with has gone off to sleep with an old lover, Dog's best mate on the island. Dog thought he'd better come up to the hut to keep me company for a while. He told me people were under the impression he'd gone to check the astronomy shed. I've been put high up on a clifftop for the night. The ham shack's a building with two mattresses on the floor. Officially, it's for amateur radio enthusiasts. Unofficially, it's for people on the station who have to get away from other people on the station. I'm in bed with Dog because I'm intrigued to be with a man who hasn't been with a woman for a very long time. And because I want to be touched. And because I have nothing to lose.

His foreplay is a rapid flick flick flick of my nipple which I'm more curious about than anything else. It's utterly unarousing. His penis hurts, it grates, I'm not wet yet and he pushes it in and then out and then harder and harder, ramming it deep inside me as far as it will go as if he wants to puncture something and I imagine that this is close to what it's like to be raped. My head bang bang bangs against the wall behind me. I cry out. He doesn't understand I'm hurting. He has no idea. He thinks it's arousal when all it is is sore. There's no tenderness. I want him to come and be done with it. The condom splits with the force of it all. He doesn't come. He flops onto his back. He says his mates will be starting to miss him and he'd better get going. He says see ya and smacks a kiss on my forehead and he's gone.

It's a night of scrawny sleep. The wind roars around me. In the cocoon of my thermal sleeping bag I can hear the sea that's bashing into the cliff below and I can hear the barks and belches of the elephant seals. I wake early and tired. There's a rawness between my legs. I remember, then, something I'd forgotten, one of the first things Dog told me when I invited him inside.

'I'm not very good with women, Fin.'

I walk outside. The orange hull's bright in the grey of the sea. The melancholy horn sounds loudly, summoning me back. I stand high on the cliff and can feel the wind and the wet bashing the city out of me, can feel it bashing away alarm clocks and deadlines and rush. I can feel, in the stiffness of my spine fighting the push of the breeze on the cliff, a readiness in me for change.

Dog seems oblivious of my response to last night as I wait for my chopper to be loaded for the flight back. He's infectiously cocky. He gives me a quick rundown of the Macca nicknames as we stand by the helipad. Rip, because he's always sleeping. Chux, because he ties his hair back with strips of Chux Superwipes. Hump, because his surname sounds a bit like a camel. Stretch, because he's tall. Dog, from grade six and he's forgotten why. I ask him about Hole.

'Aw Fin you don't want to know that one.'

'Come on, Dog.'

'It's not fit for young ladies.'

'Mate, I'm not as young as you think. And I don't know about the lady bit either.'

We grin. The ship's horn sounds again. Time to go. Dog hugs me and curls my fingers around the curved and grooved tooth of an elephant seal. He tells me to write and I say sure. I know I won't. On the chopper ride back my fingers move over the long grey tooth as if it's a chess piece, as if I'm contemplating my next move.

•

My cabin's dim and bleak. It shouts emptiness. Andrea's played cricket with Patrick and now she's sleeping with him too. Blanca's sleeping with a sailor she found in the bar. They're men with a precious commodity—a cabin to themselves. I lie on my bunk in my suddenly lonely room and have strong tugging dreams of my family and close friends and a lover I was going to marry once and I wake with a jerk and want skin to miss.

I go down to the engine room where Simeon spills the secrets of the ship to me.

'My dear, I was taught well. When I was thirty-two my mother, who'd been a Hoover house-wife all her life, got a job. For a year she paid me to stay at home and watch the midday soaps. I had to present her each night with a detailed report. I have developed an ear and an eye for signs.'

Over the muffled roar of the ship's two engines he tells me there's been speculation and rumours about every female expeditioner who's ever been to Antarctica, except for one. He tells me that after a month there are usually pairings with any single women and the other men then know not to crack onto them. He tells me that what the men hate, more than anything, is women who pick at the smorgasbord before them and move from man to man.

'The best relationships between expeditioners who are already attached in the real world are the ones where the two of them shake hands at the voyage's end and say thanks for that, it was great, have a nice life. But I've seen dreadful scenes on the wharf with the man saying goodbye to the Antarctic girlfriend, who's yelling at him, with his wife who hasn't seen him for eighteen months beside him in tears.'

'Who's the woman there's never been gossip about?'

'I'm not telling you that, my dear. You're a journalist.'

'Aw Simmy, come on.'

He holds the woman in high esteem. I'm not going to find out.

'What about homosexuality?'

The response is brisk.

'They're not that type of men, the ones that go down south.'

Half asleep on the carpet of the rec room. Listening to the slide and clank of objects in the hold. It's as though I'm pressing my head to a hungry giant's belly. I jerk awake in a big-ship tip. About twenty people in low chairs around me are watching a video and are sliding in unison two metres forward and then two metres back and then doing it all over again. It's perfectly synchronised. Someone yells to turn off the video. Watching themselves is much more fun.

Aerobics are cancelled. Doctor's orders. She doesn't want to be fixing broken limbs.

I'm sick. I took off my patch because I thought I had my sea legs. It could be seasickness but I worry that I'm pregnant. The condom split and although he didn't come, there could've been spillage and I don't want morning sickness in Antarctica and God help me I don't want a baby or an abortion. I do a sour heave into the toilet bowl and fall onto the bunk. A thudding head forces me up and there's the rush to be sick again. I go to the doctor. She doesn't seem surprised when I ask for a pregnancy test. It's negative. I go back to the cabin. Blanca beside me is also sick. Andrea's bouncily not. I put on a fresh patch and the nausea stops and Blanca asks for one too. It's my last. I hand it across.

•

WHO NEEDS LUNA PARK WHEN YOU'VE GOT OUR SHIP?

The message is large on the whiteboard when I finally make it back to the mess for a meal.

The circle of far blue horizon around the ship contracts. Snow flurries. It nestles in corners and crevices on the decks and turns the vessel into a Christmas ship. We've passed the Roaring Forties and the Furious Fifties, we've passed the sixtieth latitude. We are now in Antarctic waters.

The ship's roll stills as we sail into the thickness of mist.

FOUR

TRAPPING THE

SKY

When the mist lifts the sky is white and the ocean disappears as we sail deeper south. On the first day, the water's like heaving marble. It's grey-black, with long veins of white through it. The next day there are giant icecubes bobbing in a bathtub sea. Then it's ice pancakes. As far as I can see. Floating pancakes with their edges kicked up from nudging one another. Like an ocean of severed ears. Over the days the pancakes grow bigger and I peel off my seasickness patch. The ice has battened down the swell. I make a pilgrimage to the bridge every morning to check the changes.

'Shit, you're frightening.'

Tyrel, as I bash into him in the corridor. I didn't see him coming out of his cabin door. His knot of anger stops me still. I can't think of anything to say. I murmur sorry, quickly, and walk away.

'You should learn to fucking slow down, you maniac. You're fucking dangerous.'

The voice is as taut as stretched wire. I don't turn around.

Sun bashes my eyes, snapping them tight. The day's seared by brightness. I'm not wearing my Antarctic issue sunglasses because I want to see, unfiltered, the white around us. There are giant water lilies of ice. They're packed tight. The world's still and vivid and bright. I squint against the hurting glare.

Several hours later my eyelids can hardly open. It's as though a film of milk is over them. I panic. Blanca fetches Helen. Her diagnosis: snowblindness. The surface of my eyes has been savagely sunburnt. My temples are thudding. I have to stay in bed, in the soothing dimness of the cabin, for three days. Blanca brings chocolate biscuits and hot Milo from the mess and sings Spanish love songs to me. She's stopped going to the bar. She says a man came up to her while she was having a beer and told her God gave her feet to stand on and boobs to have sex. She didn't know what boobs were. She had to ask Jim. Blanca says she's not sure about these Australian men.

Andrea I rarely see. She's with Patrick. And she's smug.

Max visits. I ask him where Jack is and he says in their cabin and he looks surprised at my question. He brings me chocolate and reads to me from *Miss Smilla's Feeling For Snow*. I close my eyes and listen to his voice and think that Miss Smilla's like a bloke in drag. Jim visits. He brings three beers and asks for my tape recorder. He wants to take over my job while I'm stuck in my cabin. I give it to him. It could be interesting. I tell him to look after it. Callie, a student vet, visits. She describes the world outside the porthole. She says there are meringue puffs of ice with the sun glinting off them and there's a big blue sky. She reckons it's just what heaven looks like, only it'd be warmer.

I sleep scrappily. My eyes water. The milky sensation takes a long time to go away. I feel a loneliness as vast as a desert.

Snowflakes kiss my cheeks and my bare hands as I watch him.

'It's not cold. I didn't think it wouldn't be

cold,' he says as he holds his bare hand to the snow.

We're on the bow. He's got the quiet rapture of a small, grave schoolboy as he stands among the dithery flakes. He's six foot three and he's never seen snow.

Mark's home is a wilting desert town in Western Australia. He's thirty-two. He's never been beyond the borders of his State. Until now. He's a builder and he's going to Mawson Station to help with a summer building program. He looks like a scruffy Viking with his dirty blond hair to his shoulders. His voice doesn't belong to his body. It's quiet and it's careful and it betrays a deep shyness.

Mark says that when he found out he got the job, after a six-month application process, all his mates started handing him their cameras. He had requests for whales and icebergs and polar bears and every woman on the station. His best mate from primary school wanted a rock. Mark found out the day before sailing that he couldn't collect any. So after the ship left the dock he went down to the galley and got a jar from Henry the cook. He's going to fill it with Antarctic ice.

'Sure it'll melt, but when I get back to WA my mate can put it in his freezer and have a jar of

Antarctica. You should do it too, Fin. Then you'd have a chunk of Antarctica forever.'

When I come into my cabin after lunch, there's an empty jar on my pillow. Blanca winks from her bed. I tell her it's not like that with me and Mark and she says yeah darling, sure.

We're on deck making a snow woman and Mark has gone off to collect more snow when I suddenly hear softly and tenderly, hey there, as if he's speaking to a lover. I turn. Mark's crouching in a corner and he stands up with something squawking and biting and attacking his chest. Hey there, hey there. It's a small bird. It's snowy white, with a pitch black beak and feet. It's young and panicking.

'Thank God I'm not a woman,' says Mark as the bird works itself into a frenzy with the material of his parka across his chest.

It's a snow petrel. They've replaced the albatrosses circling the ship now that we've hit the ice. The birds call and dip and soar like angels in the sky around us. The one in Mark's hands struggles and squawks and spits green slime down his parka. I laugh. Mark doesn't. I tell him to put it down. It shouldn't be held. It sits on the snow very still, quietly trembling. It makes a ratchety sound in the back of its beak, as if it's trying to bring up phlegm.

'Something's terribly wrong for it not to be flying,' I say.

Mark picks it up and the beak goes again and he puts it back in the sheltered corner where he found it. He gets me to sit in the snow by the bird while he tracks down William who's studying snow petrels on the continent. The bird presses itself into the corner away from me. I move away from it. William arrives and says hello my fellow and picks it up with swift, sure hands. He spreads its wings wide one after the other and feels carefully along their span. He can't find anything wrong. He tells us to throw it overboard and see how it goes. I say it can't fly. He looks at me dubiously.

'You want to look after it?'

I don't. I've got too much work to do. I say yes. William tells me to get some raw seafood from Henry the cook.

Night. The bridge. Just Max, Jack and me, and Ivan, the officer on watch. The room's lights are off. The bridge's circumference seems to have shrunk about us in the almost-dark. We stand close.

Our skin's coloured a soft green by the glow from the computers and radar screens. I feel drawn into the comfortable stillness. We look out into the night. Two spotlights are high on the bow. They're like World War Two searchlights sending long, shining paths ahead of us. Snow speeds horizontally like bullets through their brightness.

'No other ship I know has headlights,' says Ivan, his voice sudden in the dark. 'Every other ship is in darkness at night, so it can see any other lights around it. But not us. In Antarctica we have to be able to see the ice. That's why we have headlights, Fin. Oh, look, the radar says an iceberg. Maybe . . . half an hour away.'

Ivan points to a blip of green on the screen. It's the first iceberg of the voyage. Ivan's bemused at our excitement. The blip moves slowly towards the centre of the screen. The ship surges ahead in the blackness. Max ducks downstairs to get his camera. He returns as Jack begins yelling and pointing.

A bump in the distance, port side. Ivan traps the berg and holds it, theatrically, in the spotlight. The ship veers and comes up close. The cliff of ice reminds me of passing a tanker. The weather has sculpted turrets and hollows and spires. The berg's a ghostly lime-green in the light. It's so still. So utterly, terribly lifeless. I feel as though the ship's an intruder in this strange, other world that we have no right to be in.

Max braves outside in a thin shirt. He wants to see his first iceberg without the barrier of thick glass. He yells at me to come too. I stay inside. I've gorged myself with imagining being with him and now it's all gone. I suspect he's gay. I'd be mad to go out on deck in my shirt.

An announcement's put over the intercom. Suddenly there are people and pyjamas and binoculars and cameras and lights and exclamations all around us.

A sweep's been held to guess the timing of the first iceberg sighting. Andrea's closest. She's with Patrick. I tell the capain that I'll deliver her box of wine. I don't know if he knows. I take the box back to the cabin and put it on Andrea's bed and imagine what she's doing at this very moment.

I go to sleep thinking of cliffs of ice and the sweet softness of skin to skin.

The bird demands with its stillness. I feed it krill collected by the marine biologists on the trawl deck of the ship, and galley scraps from Henry. It gets to know the smell of my arrival. It turns its head keenly and, eventually, without trembling. I won't let it take the meat from my fingers. I don't trust its beak. I worry about the stillness of its wings. It lives in a cardboard fruit box on a mattress of snow in a sheltered corner of the deck. William tells me it'll leave when it's able. Callie picks it up. Says maybe it has concussion.

'It's so young. Its wings haven't fully formed. Maybe the wind bashed it into the side of the ship during a fog. It's lucky it fell onto the deck and you two found it.'

She tells me it's a he. She christens it Fin-tu.

'Fin number two. Because you're obsessed by him.'

'No I'm not. It's just that I like his company. We sit here by ourselves and watch the ice.'

She looks at me and shakes her head. 'You city girls are very strange.'

Mark comes and sits quietly beside us. We stare out at the wide ice that's impersonating land and he talks about the desert. How he used to play footy for his local town and his father trained him, put him in army boots and made him run ten kilometres a day behind the ute.

'Walking and jogging and sprinting in these
great big bloody boots, and then when I got onto
the field, with the football boots on, I felt like I
was dancing. I felt like a bloody ballerina!'

Blanca comes and sits beside me and pulls out
a cigarette. I tell her to go away. The smoke stains
the crisp cold air. She hovers, fidgety and not really
listening, for ten minutes or so and then she's gone,
pulling out a cigarette and trailing smoke in her
wake.

I sit and feed Fin-tu and watch the bergs go
by. They're so dignified. Some are like Walt Disney
castles or pooltables or Cambodian temples or
Uluru. One day we pass one that's so blue, it's as
if its ice has captured a piece of the sky inside it.

I lean back and close my eyes in the sun. It's
red and warm and bright under my eyelids and I
put my hands behind my head. I feel a tugging at
my pocket. Fin-tu's under my arm. He has a piece
of krill in his sharp black beak.

'You little bugger.'

The tape recorder's on the bunk when I walk into
the cabin. Jim dropped it off. The cassette I left in
it is gone. I pick up the machine and check it. The

cassette wheel spins and whirs to a stop. Jim's run down the batteries. I check the battery meter. It tells me the batteries are okay, but I change them anyway. I press play and the cassette slows and stops again, as if it's run out of puff. I try to shake away its weariness. I press play. Nothing happens. It's stuffed. It's the only tape recorder I have on the voyage, the single most precious item I'm carrying with me. I'm only halfway through interviewing the people I want to on the ship and I haven't even got to Antarctica. Fuck him. I stride down the corridor, my face tight.

He's lying on his bunk reading a porn mag.

'Aw, Fin, I'm sorry.' He smiles his sweet smile. 'I just thought it was me, that's why I didn't tell you. I thought I was pressing the wrong buttons. Mate, everything breaks in Antarctica. And the bugger is, I didn't even get a chance to do any interviews for you. There goes my brilliant career. Hey, have a beer, mate, sit down, you look as if you've just fought a bushfire.'

I tell him it's a fucking problem because I'm getting paid to do a job down here and now, thanks to him, I can't do it. I ask him what the fuck he's going to do about it. He snaps upright on his bed.

'Fin, we'll get it fixed. We'll put a notice up

in the mess. One of the boffins'll know what to do.'

William, the snow petrel biologist, comes hesitantly to me and tells me that years ago he worked in a radio repair shop. He can't promise anything. He takes my machine and with delicate pianist's fingers unscrews the back and carefully picks out the machine's guts so that a mass of red and green and white wire entrails spill from it. He picks at and rearranges the wires. After a very long time William finally looks up and declares the machine, tentatively, fixed.

I kiss him on both cheeks and he flushes deeply, first his neck, then his whole face. He says he loves fixing things, that it's nothing special.

I continue my work. My aim is to eventually capture almost everyone on the ship: why they're here, how it's working out, what they're missing. Jim catches me interviewing Mark in a quiet corner of the rec room. His voice comes in over the top of our talk.

'I thought I'd fixed that thing once and for all.'

I turn off the tape recorder.

'Mate, go away. You've already done enough damage.'

He smiles and blows me a kiss.

In a slice of a room in the belly of the ship I find
a place to be alone. The gym. I'm in there every
day. I wear my pyjama shorts and a T-shirt and
turn the music up loud. It's like a glass of wine
after a frantic day. I begin to crave it.

Tyrel finds it.

He begins to come in the middle of my ses-
sions and there's nothing I can do to stop him. I
snap off the sound and leave soon after he enters.

I stop going and begin pacing the deck instead.
I'm always checking on Fin-tu. He's getting cheek-
ier. He knows I mean meat and he can read the
sound of my footsteps. Sometimes he'll chatter in
his ratchety voice and spit and stretch out his wings
and fold them back in again. He never makes an
attempt to fly. I don't want him to now.

In a flat patch of ice, Adélie penguins scurry
from the slice of the ship. They leave tracks in the
ice like lines on a hand. In a channel between floes
there are Minke whales, their deep grey backs
breaking the water's surface in a calm arc.

I walk the decks. Mark comes up often to
check on Fin-tu, as do William and Callie. I stop

and chat and walk the decks again. I stand still on the helideck and curl my fingers into the mesh of the tall fence and put my face to the cold wire. My body weight bounces on the fence, challenges the tension. I'd last less than a minute in the water.

Tyrel's suddenly behind me, on the far side of the deck. His small tight figure is hunched into his parka. I imagine him pushing me overboard. It'd be twelve hours or more before anyone would realise I was missing and it'd be quick and so easy. The perfect crime. A thrillingly glamorous way to go. I walk to another deck and lean over the railing and water gushes up from the split in the ice below me, like blood from a deep wound.

I'd thought about suicide once, long ago, when a relationship broke apart three weeks before we were going to marry. I'd thought of jumping from my high apartment window, of striding into the sky. I look back now and think how stupid it was, to think of doing that, for a man. But I'd wanted him so savagely haunted.

I think about that line from *Huckleberry Finn*, 'I felt so lonesome I most wished I was dead', as I kneel in the snow on the very tip of the bow under a sky that's thick with stars. I listen. There's the soft whoosh of the splitting ice below me, its protesting squeak and plup as it buckles under the insistent iron. I watch a hairline crack in the ice journey far and split wide as the ship cuts its course.

There's a shooting star, and then another. There's no wind. I feel like we're sailing into a silent and strange place where we've no right to be. Cold creeps into my clothes and I go below.

Tyrel looks up from inside his cabin as I pass his open door. He watches me.

Ivan puts Mozart on loud and sails into a headwind to protect us during our barbecue on the trawl deck. The deck's low, at the rear of the ship. It's −15°C. There's a velvet blanket of a sunset sky. Among the expeditioners there are Rudolph red noses and difficulties in negotiating sausage sandwiches with woollen gloves on.

'I reckon this would have to be the only Aussie barbie I've ever been to that doesn't have flies,' Max says. He fishes out a chocolate bar from Jack's pocket and tells me I have to eat it because it's energy food and a vital staple of an expeditioner's diet. He tries to force it into my mouth.

I hit him with the back of my hand across his chest and we laugh and stare out at the icebergs. He goes to get another sausage sandwich. Blanca sidles up beside me and tells me she's not seeing her sailor anymore. All she will tell me is that she's too clever to love him. She won't say who he is.

Andrea's not at the barbecue. Neither's Tyrel. While Jim tells me about plans for a talent night and how his stereo and walkman and watchstrap are all broken, I look across at Max. He's laughing with Callie in a corner. He offers her some chocolate. She takes it. Maybe he isn't gay. Jim drifts away.

Gino comes up to me.

'Hey, birdwoman!'

He untwists his beer bottle cap in his eye socket. He wants to show me photos of his family. Gino's surname is Fortunasso and his Antarctic nickname is Lucky Bum. He's a diesel mechanic and he's twenty-four, the youngest tradie on the ship. In his cabin I learn a new word. Stickmags. Porn magazines. Gino has a lot. I want to have a look but he pushes his photo album under my nose. There are stern wedding photos of his parents and snaps of his sisters and his boat and his hotted up

V8 in the driveway of a large brick suburban home. There are lots of photos of his two year old niece.

'She's my baby.'

We chat for a while about nothing much, then he puts the album away.

'What I do feel, Fin, is that Antarctica is going to change me. It's this really strange feeling. I've never had it before. Getting this job is the biggest thing that's ever happened to me.' He talks about his father who came to Australia from Malta in 1949 and worked long days and nights as a mechanic and eventually lost all the sensitivity in his fingers through years of accumulated grease and it was like that for a very long time; then one day his father came home from work and cleaned his fingers with olive oil and sugar and he got his touch back. After Gino's story we look at each other and smile.

'I've been told that everyone comes back from Antarctica a different person.'

'Hey, me too, Fin. Do you ever get that feeling that your life hasn't really begun? That it's all supposed to start next month or next year, but it never does, kind of?'

The ocean's black ink between the floes. Clean, cold air is like a tonic in my lungs after the warm insides of Gino's cabin. The night's soaked in still-ness. The world around me seems snap-frozen. I make my way to Fin-tu. Just in time to see a figure bending over his box, picking up his feathery flap-ping whiteness in clumsy outstretched hands and a man striding to the railing and my voice my body is caught with the shock and I don't move and I don't speak until his arms are out over the rails.

'Tyrel!'

I rush forward, my heart whamming in my chest, and he turns and tells me it'll be better off in its own world and he can't bear to watch it anymore and as I say don't! his hands throw Fin-tu out and away and down and I'm leaning far over the railing with my feet on the bottom rung and Fin-tu is dropping and trying to work his wings and dropping and dropping as the ship moves swiftly on and is gone.

I don't cry. I'm very calm. There's a core of ice-composure within me.

'He'll be much better off down there,' says Tyrel. It's like there's an anger in his chest as tight and as hard as a tinfoil ball.

My face feels very set and very old as I turn and look at him, then walk away.

Blanca draws up the blankets and kisses me on the forehead like my mother used to. I turn to the wall and feel a sudden hot rush behind my eyes. I don't cry. I don't sleep for a very long time. When I finally do, I dream I'm sleeping with my eyes wide open. Or maybe I am.

Meg's a woman who absorbs secrets. She doesn't smile with her mouth open. She grins and it never seems generous. Her teeth are like chips of amber. She's a vet, the senior woman on the voyage who's been down south several times before. She's fierce at the helm of what she calls a get-together for the women on the ship. To discuss 'female issues'. I want to record it but I don't dare ask. I settle for a notepad instead.

She tells us to remember there are no secrets in Antarctica. She tells us we'll have to get used to pissing and shitting in company if we're going to be camping in the field. She tells us plastic bags are for solid waste, and plastic film cartridges are good for tampons.

'What's that like, going to the toilet in front of the guys on your team?' asks Callie.

'Well, they don't exactly stand around and watch. It's just done. Everyone's got bodily functions. If you're at all inhibited about that sort of thing, you're in the wrong place.'

Anya, a biologist, wants to go on the pill to stop herself menstruating in the field. She thinks it'll be too messy to have to deal with, and too smelly. Helen says it's not such a good idea. She says the pill will create a buildup in her uterus, and she could get irregular and continual bleeding. Not good, on the ice.

'Dammit', Anya says.

Meg tells us not to leave going to the toilet to the last minute because we'll have up to six layers of Antarctic gear on and it takes time to get it off. She says soggy accidents aren't fun. She says to remind the men we need a bit more time than them.

'They can just whip it out and go, but for us, it takes a bit longer.'

'I can do it quickly,' says Andrea. 'My mother taught me to urinate standing up when I was little. She told me it was something to do with the way men treat women, some sort of statement.'

The rest of the women laugh. I've said nothing

in the meeting. My mind's weighted down with thinking about Fin-tu. I scribble his head, again and again, on my notepad.

Meg declares the meeting closed and asks me to stay back.

'I heard you had a bit of a run-in with Tyrel. Don't think too much about it. He's a good man. He did what he thought was right.'

She has the calm of experience in her. Her calm's no comfort. I smile and tell her thank you, okay, yeah. I ask her how she knew about Fin-tu going overboard and she says remember, there are no secrets in Antarctica. She says it's all around the ship and that dwelling on things in Antarctica can create a lot of problems. She says once a deed is done, that's it, move on, don't look back, because a lot of things don't turn out the way you want them to down south. As she walks out of the room she tells me to keep smiling.

'You have such a beautiful smile, Fin. It's a real gift. It lights up your whole face.'

A cluster of birds follows the ship like children from Hamelin. They feast on the krill that's kicked up by the hull as it chops through the ice. Sometimes there are so many birds it's like something out of Hitchcock. Gradually I stop looking for Fin-tu among them all.

The floes change. From a bumpy jostling white moonscape to motionless, flat sheets as big as ice-rinks.

I busy myself with interviews. There are early morning satellite connections to Australia for crosses into current affairs programs. I've got commitments with radio stations across Australia, doing live-to-air chats on the satellite phone. The line costs nine dollars a minute but the stations don't seem to care. The listeners, they tell me, are hungry for Antarctica. I speak to the program producers before going to air and dictate the questions the announcers will ask me. My answers are rough on a notepad in front of me. The challenge is to always sound fresh when up to ten different stations are getting the same yarn. The more serious current affairs programs get me to fax detailed introductions and questions and rough outlines of what my spontaneous sounding answers are going to be.

And there are news stories. Two paragraph intros and thirty-second voice reports, summing up the various scientific projects on the voyage. I file my work early because the big morning bulletins are the most listened to ones of the day and I want my stories in them.

I rise and watch dawn skies that look like they're veiled in thin muslin. I do my work and then drink cups of tea with Captain Crane on the bridge and he tells me about his daughters and his wife and his home in Broome and we stare at the many shades of white around us. Max is often up early too. He tells me the Inuit have forty words for white and I begin to see them all. Max asks me why I've been avoiding him lately. I tell him I haven't, I've just been busy.

At night I listen on my tape recorder to the voices I've collected. They're for documentary specials I'll package up on my return. The recordings are never captured cleanly, there's always the hum of the ship's engine under them. I read the people in their voices. In Max's voice there's sharpness, a keen curiosity. It's someone who doesn't suffer fools gladly. In Jim, there's bluff, something that warns me away, something that doesn't like women. In Mark, a wanting to please. In Blanca, a fear of her accent. In Andrea, shyness. In Meg, wariness, a lack of confidence. In Jack, a wanting the journalist to go away and leave him alone. In the voice asking the questions, a little girl. I sound ten years younger than I am. It's not my real voice. It's how I operate. Playing naive and ingenuous, charming people into dropping their guard. The voice is light and high, playacting, and I can hardly bear to listen to it. I snap the tape recorder off and suddenly the sounds of the ship in the night are loud and boomy and raucous about me.

There are rumours of couples in the darkroom, a lab, a helicopter. I wonder whether Callie and Max are together somewhere.

I volunteer for slushy duty in the kitchen. It's fun and chatty and wet and the cooks and the stewards are a good source of information. Two hundred and eighty dishes are washed with a high pressure hose in a single sitting and I'm soaking wet and knobbly-kneed at the end of it. The kitchen staff applaud as I leave.

They want to shave my head. It's a ship tradition. I tell them I need my hair to keep me warm and I suggest Gino instead. They corner him in the bar. He says no bloody way. The crew suggest a compromise with his beard.

'You're not getting that. I couldn't bear to face

104

myself in the mirror every morning without my beard covering me up. Pick on someone else.'

Mark agrees to a public shaving on the trawl deck. With his long hair gone, he loses, stunningly, his looks. Andrea records the step-by-step transformation with her camera. At the end of it, I give Mark my beanie to keep himself warm. He puts it on and smiles thank you.

Henry asks me to be a judge at the upcoming talent night. I'm flattered. He says he'll dress me. He tells me to go up and look at the ice before I do the dishes.

'There's a floe out there four kilometres across, Fin. It's as big as a suburb.'

I stare at virgin-smooth ice through my glacier goggles. A snow petrel dips and soars around the ship. I'm sure Fin-tu's dead.

FIVE

SCRUBBED

EYEBALLS

Two black garbage bags are wrapped around my body. Masking tape in thick brown bands is strapping the plastic to me. Makeup is thick on my skin, I can feel the texture of it, the dryness. I haven't worn makeup since Macquarie Island. It feels like a mask. I wear Henry's blonde party wig and high shoes with thin heels. I step from behind two shower curtains limp with age and the scum of old soap. They're strung, sagging, together. I step through the curtains to a wall of applause and wolf whistles and cheers. Men crowd to me. William swears he'll never wash his arm again as I scrawl a heart in marking pen on his outstretched skin. Jim flips up his shirt. I scribble on his back. He moans and tells me to do it again. I laugh and push him away. I'm a visiting pop star, the talent night's celebrity judge. I step in my spindly heels through the crowd in the bar to my plastic chair of honour.

Eyes are staring at my chest. My hand flutters across my breasts. My fingers tug at the plastic hem of my dress.

The quest begins. There are guitars and a violin and a hearty singalong and jokes. There's a beer break and the lights come up and Steve the sailor MC turns his back to the audience and drops his pants. There's a flash of startled white flesh and the shadow of his hairy balls between his legs. There are groans and screams and yells to get him off. Someone throws an empty beer can at him. The lights are dimmed. There are more jokes and then Max steps from behind the shower curtain. He's kitted out in full Antarctic gear with an icepick in his hands. He's a British wildlife documentary host. He's investigating the strange species known as Antarctican Australis.

'These people have undergone a multitude of tests. They've had blood tests, ECGs, psychiatry tests, they've had their bank account names and numbers recorded as well as their shoe, hand and head size and their inside leg measurement. These people are the selected elite—you just wouldn't know it by looking at them.'

And it goes on. At the end of the skit I hold my scorecard up high. Fourteen out of ten. There's loud approval and a fresh round of drinking and jokes and another song. The night grows ragged.

The last act. Gino and the stickmag boys. A borrowed black bra is dangled across the bar's television. On it, with the volume down, is a soft core porn flick. In front of it there are self-conscious tradies who can't quite remember their lines. The skit crawls, the audience begins to rustle, talk bubbles up. Then there's a punch of laughter when from behind the shower curtains steps, magnificently, The Journalist. The crowd's wilting focus is snapped to attention. Laughter comes and comes. It dumps me like a wave.

It's Jim. In his hand is a carrot spearing an orange. It's his microphone. He wears my signature black reporter's clothes. He has on sunglasses and red lipstick that's smeared and leering behind a blond scrap of a new beard. His hair is in bits of high pigtails. My polo neck's straining across an enormous chest with fifties cone breasts.

The laughter goes on and on. My hand flutters across my chest. I feel prickly and wrong in the dress. I want to get out. I laugh.

Jim flounces in front of the crowd and adjusts

his breasts and asks naive and nagging questions
to the faces at the front. Onya Stiffy, someone yells.
He pushes his microphone at them. He adjusts his
breasts and runs his finger up his thigh and opens
his mouth and runs his tongue around his lips. He
speaks to the expeditioners in a girly voice that
veers high into a tone that is, at times, exactly like
mine.

'You're dead, Jim, you're dead.'

My laughing twin tone reaches to him over
the thickness of the noise around us. The skit skids.
Jim stumbles over my outstretched foot as he leaves
and the crowd screams laughter again and I'm
laughing too as I hold up the scorecard. Minus
6,072. The crowd whistles and claps loud approval
and Max gets the bottle of wine and Steve the MC
turns and chucks another brown eye and the talent
night is ended and the lights come on bright and
the spectators see me laughing and laughing as I
push my way swiftly out.

In the shower's strong water I scrub at the makeup
and the sticky branding of the masking tape under
my arms and across the top of my breasts and then
I sag to the shower wall and put my wet cheek to

it and tears and water are spilling down and my body slides to the small plastic floor tray and I stay hunched in its palm for a very long time, weeping and weeping until I finally stop. I turn off the water. I'm still and wet and cold for what seems like a very long time.

My Grand Canyon weeping. It feels as though there are years of not crying in it, as though it's all, finally, rushing out. I'm used to holding things in, several ex-boyfriends have pointed it out. 'There's a tightness to you,' said the fiancé, as he left, 'let it all out.' And now I am. I feel like a good expeditioner, doing exactly what the Antarctic Survival Guide says to: Don't bottle things up, don't simmer.

The cabin's thick with quiet when I step from the bathroom. My face feels plumped under the surface with tears as I fall quickly to my bed. I don't want any eyes, I don't want looking.

'Oh Fin, they were so *mean* to you.'

Andrea. There's a gloat in there somewhere, in the back of her voice. Blanca's silent. I know it must have been her that supplied the polo neck. Fuck it. When the blow comes, it's so often not from enemies but from those who are closest to you. I turn to the wall and the hot quick tears come silently again. A careful stillness is in the cabin around me.

'Darling, I did not realise they would do what they did,' says Blanca suddenly into the quiet.

'It's okay.'

'I had no idea—'

'It's okay.'

I turn to her with a smile that collects my face and my voice. 'It's okay, really.'

I can't bring myself to call her darling. There's a festive knock. Blanca fortresses the cabin door with her bulk. Her body's brisk, as if she's wanting to make up for it all. It's Jim. Smeared cherry-red rims his mouth ridiculously.

'Not now. I'll talk to you tomorrow, Jim.'

There's a new voice in me. There's no welcome in it and a deep tiredness and an oldness. I recognise, startled, my mother in the voice. My face turns back to the wall and the blankets are drawn close around my shoulders. There's no talk between Blanca and Andrea. I don't know what their faces are saying. There's another knock.

'Go *away*,' I say loudly as Blanca opens the door.

It's Max.

'Hey Fin, I'm going outside to have a look at the stars. Wanna come?'

We climb high to a star-crammed sky. The world outside seems to have stopped, it's glistening and crunchy as we walk across the decks and climb steel ladders to the very tip of the bow. We say nothing. There's a clarity to the sound of our feet on the hardened snow; the noises are strangely new and magnified and crisp. As if during the day they fray, competing with all the other noises, and they need soothing night to become fresh again.

Max points to a satellite moving calmly among the stars. It's stately on its slow path.

'You know, Jim reminds me of my next-door neighbour when I was a kid. He was the star of the street, Fin, but it was like, everyone loved him except for his family. They couldn't stand him.'

I smile.

'Are you okay?'

'Yeah.'

I laugh. I feel as though I'm young and over-reacting and silly. 'I've just got to toughen up I suppose. You know, Max, I think I'm really strong and grownup but I'm not. You know, the big tough journo thing. I'm just not.'

Ivan trains the spotlight on us. We turn,

rabbited, in the strong track of light and laugh and wave and throw snowballs at the far bridge windows. The snow falls well short of its target. We go down below.

In the mess Max makes me a hot Milo. We drink the warmth in our cups under too-bright lights. It's midnight. We say goodnight and go off to our beds.

The morning staggers. I pass Tyrel in the corridor and he smiles, friendly and soft and in sympathy. I can't smile back. I turn from the door to the mess. I can't face breakfast and the faces, the stickmag men's faces. I feel shrivelled.

'Don't be intimidated by the boys, darling, whatever it is happens. My response would be to push my, what is it, boobs, right in their face. They want to see you down.'

Blanca, standing tall before me on my return to the cabin. I can't put my breasts in their faces, I don't have the courage or the will for it. I mask my body in obscuring layers and wear my hair plain in a low ponytail with a centre part. My face can't smile. My eyes are scratchy from tears. I can't stop my face, I can't stop the tears.

Hunger pushes me to lunch. There's a trail of a tear over the soup, it slips into a fragile dangle on the end of my nose. Splashes. Dents the thickness of the soup. I rise swiftly from someone's midsentence and Helen's quickly behind me in the corridor.

'I hope you're not upset by that business last night. It's just men. It wasn't aimed at you, it was about women in general. They get excitable. It's the hormones. And it just goes to show, Fin, that you're popular. They'd only do it to someone they thought could take it.'

I can hear the tone in her voice telling me to pull myself together. I force a breezy smile. 'No, no, I'm not upset. Really.'

Afternoon, in the computer room. I transcribe interviews with my back to everyone. They don't see the thin trails of mucus from my nose, or the sleeves of my skivvy near my wrists that are spiderwebbed with snot.

A thick corded arm extends over my shoulder. A Toblerone bar is placed on my notepad.

'I thought you might need it.'

Softly.

The arm retreats. I half turn my head. It's Max. I can't look him in the eye to say thank you.

•

We're standing on an icefloe that's fifteen metres wide. A chunk of ice floating on the Great Southern Ocean. Giant tiles of ice are ahead of and beside us, stretching as far as we can see. And then, almost imperceptibly, there's a swell, like a giant's slumbering breathing. Max looks across at me and sticks up his thumb and smiles.

I carry two screwdrivers in my pockets. They're attached by ropes to my clothing. If I fall through the ice I'm to use the screwdrivers to haul myself out of the water. I'll only survive a minute in it. Meg fell in last year. It took her thirty seconds to scramble out.

A crane has lifted me high in a cargo cage over the side of the ship and placed me with a thud on the snow. I'm going to record the sounds of a seal capture. A team of ten expeditioners is to throw a net over a basking crabeater seal, then wrestle it still, dope it and glue a plastic box onto its back, then let it go. The box will be tracked by a satellite that sends its data to a computer in Paris. The aim's to monitor the behavioural patterns of the crabeaters. They're the most elusive and unstudied of the seals, because they live entirely in the water or on the floating pack ice around Antarctica. The head of the team is Jack. Max is working with him, helping out as a volunteer. He's taken leave from his desk job to give Jack a hand. And to see Antarctica. Max got me onto the ice.

I switch on the tape recorder in its esky.

Beside me on the floe eight people are lying on top of a seal. It's two metres long and it's struggling violently. It's barking and huffing and growling. There's a lot of fuck fuck fuck and shit and Jesus Christ and hold him from the men, and the rip of their thin white camouflage suits in the strain of forcing the animal still. Finally, the seal's stopped. There's quiet. Someone says thank the Lord for small mercies. Meg, the team vet, comes up close and in a swift action the needle's in deep.

The people holding the seal fall back. The animal's slow, loud, laboured breathing sounds human, tenderly so, as it surrenders to the anaesthetic and is vastly asleep.

'Under,' says Meg crisply, checking and clicking her stopwatch with a snap.

A thick sludge of superglue is hurriedly mixed with a painter's trowel and caked in a slab on the seal's furry back. A plumber and a diesel mechanic and two electricians kneel in the snow and blow the glue dry. Their concentrating, panicked lips blow faster and faster as the seal groggily comes out of the anaesthetic quicker than expected. Max stands with a pen and clipboard above them, his forehead set with tension. Jack's quiet, at the seal's head.

The glue's dry. The seal comes fully up. It blinks big eyes at us all and lumbers slowly across to its mate who's been scared across to the next floe. There's relieved laughter. Max comes across to me and hits me softly on the shoulder. I stop the recorder. Cameras click and whir and there's a shout from above. We turn. The orange side of the ship looms large. Spectators line the rim of the bow like tin soldiers. Jim's one of them and he holds a cardboard scorecard high. EIGHT. There's laughter and more camera clicks and I turn and walk away. Jim and I ignore each other now.

In ten minutes I'll be back on the ship. I want to savour for just a little while standing on the patchwork quilt of ice over the ocean's surface. The floe feels solid. I walk across it. Then fall with surprise from concrete hard snow into deep soft-ness. There's a sudden panic as I plunge to my thigh into slush.

I hope Jim isn't looking.

I follow quickly after, in the footsteps of others.

•

Payback takes two passionfruit positioned carefully in a pair of men's swimmers, some persuasion from several women on the ship, and courage. I'm not sure how much I've got when I make the decision to get Jim back.

My ammunition's a pillow for a beer gut, a texta beard from Blanca, Jim's North Queensland holiday resort T-shirt procured from his delighted bunkmate, a baseball cap back to front, Jim's ever-present video camera, shorts, and over them speedos stretched tight. In them are two passionfruit, handpicked and polished by Henry the cook.

'Excuse me,' says Mark as his fingers fumble under the swimmers and jiggle the passionfruit into position. I try not to giggle. It feels good. He gives me a lesson on how a man scratches his balls.

'That's it. Just sort of reposition them. Try again. Yeah.'

As I walk out the door of my cabin Mark hands me a pile of stickmags. 'They're not mine, they're from the bunkmate.'

I laugh. 'I believe you.'

Blanca gives me advance reports. Expeditioners have crowded the rec room for my talk. Several people have requested that I fill in a slide-show spot with a lecture on my profession. I ummed and aahed because I'm good at blushing in public. The talent night decided me, though, and I walk into the expectant room. As Jim. The room erupts. Laughter comes at me and lifts me high. I drop the stickmags and aim the video camera and mimic his voice and scratch the balls and at the end of it present the real Jim with his honorary testicles.

'They should have been rockmelons, mate.'

'Well actually, Stiff, we tried jellybeans at first but they disappeared.'

I recognise behind his grin the dazed shock that I'd felt four days ago. His grin's fixed. It's a king-hit. I go outside and change my clothes and Blanca wipes off the beard and Mark takes away the men's clothes and I return to the room and talk to the expeditioners about press conferences and police scanners and microphones and deadlines and cadets. I sense surprise and attention and there's laughter through it and long warm applause at the end of it. People crowd around me.

'I'm so glad you did that. It had to be done. A lot of us wouldn't be brave enough,' says Meg. She's grinning like a split watermelon. It's damn good to see it.

Max steps up to me. 'You're the hero of the ship, Fin.'

Blanca hugs me. 'Your face is a new face, darling. It is so open and alive. It is very different. It is very good.'

Andrea, behind her, says nothing.

The ship slides up to a floe and the white-suited gladiators are dropped overboard again. The seal's quickly caught and we cheer like football spectators on the bow. Then grow quiet as we watch Meg on the ice suddenly pumping the animal's tail. She does it for a very long time. Then she stops and falls into a crouch in the snow beside the still seal. Jack swiftly drops next to her. The rest of the capture team step back. Blunt words are spoken by Jack from the ice to the ship via the walkie-talkie. They're relayed quickly among the expeditioners. The animal has died.

The seal's limp body is cradled in a net and swung high onto the trawl deck. A postmortem's to be carried out. A crowd gathers on the deck. Max's eyes don't see me when I smile my sympathy to him. Meg tells the crowd to move on. Her voice is tight.

'It's nature,' someone says loudly. But the crowd reluctantly drifts.

Max, drained, tells me later in the corridor that when the flesh of the belly was slit the vets discovered the animal was a pregnant female three weeks away from pupping. He doesn't say anything more and there are tears in his eyes and a great heaviness and weariness about him.

'Oh Max. I'm so sorry.'

'We think it was the trauma of the capture program. You know, the corralling of the seal, the net and the wrestling it still. It's pretty brutal stuff.'

The seal was sticking close to her partner. The gladiator capturers had to work hard to separate the two of them. The male hung around, persistent and panicked, after the capture of his mate. Max had to stand over him, to stop him from coming too close.

That night, the team leaders talk to a crowded rec room about what went wrong. Several expeditioners have demanded it. Jack briefly introduces Meg. He's businesslike, saying she's the expert and should be doing the explaining. He steps away as she stands.

'What happens is, when the seals are caught they go into a dive reflex. It's a natural thing.' Her voice lowers. Someone yells for her to speak up. She takes a big breath.

'When they're diving, they shut their system down. They stop breathing and pool their blood into a central cavity. The animal went into a dive reflex when we caught it, and it didn't come out of it. I was pumping its tail to try and get the blood circulating through it again. But when I checked its gums, they were blue. They weren't pink, they were blue and . . . and . . . I knew then . . . that it was . . . dead.'

Her voice rises high and it skids from control and she weeps.

'I'm sorry, this is very distressing for me. It's such an . . . an . . . honour to work with wildlife.'

There's a thud in her saying of honour. A curious politeness stills the audience. Meg struggles to contain the spill of her weeping. No-one moves to her. Transfixed, we watch. I go up and hug her when the talk's over. Mark and I are the only people around her. Many expeditioners are in knots of tight talking as they leave the room. I can't see Max. Jack is deep in conversation with Captain Crane. I know that in the kitchen the crew are saying that the animal has been killed deliberately. That the boffins did it to take a look at what was inside it. The weeping doesn't change their thinking.

The death is debated by a government ethics committee in Australia. After three hours the committee faxes through its verdict: the project can continue, in the interests of science. The carcass is kept on board for research. The ship feels weighted by the corpse.

Nothing and everything happens on the night of the four auroras.

We come looking for each other and meet on the stairwell. The evening's sliding into perfect conditions for viewing the southern lights, the strange optic phenomenon that neither of us has yet seen. We have a pact that the next time there's an aurora, we're going to photograph it. We want to trap it forever on film. Tonight, says the sky.

We retreat to our cabins to dress. I put on seven layers instead of five. The cold outside is bone deep. The chart on the bridge tells me it's −47°C with the windchill factor.

We climb metal ladders to the sky. On one side, just, there's the remnants of a sunset. On the other, against the darkness, there's the beginning glow of an aurora, its promise. We stand still and quiet and the sky darkens from plum to ink and the aurora stirs and begins to dance, like a giant scribble of moving light in the sky. He shouts, there's another—at the opposite end of the sky, a billowing green curtain—and then I shout because there's another and another. Four auroras at once, fading and pulsing back, falling like patches of green rain on the high window of the sky. The two of us are jumping and shouting and laughing and pulling each other under another bit of sky and another and then we stop, raptured under it, then we're businesslike and setting up our cameras on a railing and cold is trying to get into me, I can feel it, the hard wind. We take our pictures and he's standing in front of me and taking my hands between his gloves and pressing them with great concentration and he's rubbing my upper arms and hugging me warm, hugging away the hurting cold, and then we're sitting quiet against a sheltered wall and I'm between his legs, my back is to him and his arms are around me tight as we watch our drive-in in the sky.

The insistent cold forces us below to our narrow bunks. Max doesn't touch me goodnight, doesn't kiss, just says see ya.

It makes me know, absolutely, that I want him. That he's not gay.

It's an achingly crisp blue day and the air seems so clean it hurts. Everything outside is so hard-edged and defined, it's as if I've got new glasses with a too-strong prescription. The hurting light pushes me back inside, from the deck to the bridge.

'I feel like my eyeballs have been scrubbed,' Mark says. We commiserate over our aching sight and put on our sunglasses inside.

Max comes in, with Jack. There's no signal of the everything of last night. Maybe he was just warming me, nothing more than that. There's no flicker of a sign in his public greeting. Okay, so he was just warming me.

I don't ask anything, I bounce back offhandedness in my greeting to them both. I move to another corner, contracting inside, not risking rejection and humiliation, not risking. He was just warming me.

It hurts. I have to leave. I walk out of the room. I feel foolish and naive. I hear footsteps behind me in the corridor. I turn. Max catches me up.

While Jack's at lunch Max reads aloud to me on the couch in his cabin. From *The Little Prince*. He relishes the speaking parts. I laugh. My concentration wanders and comes back and I get him to repeat the lines that I want to hear again. My arms are around my bunched knees beside him. He's leaning against my arm. His skin is against mine. It feels natural; it makes me not want to move. He's stroking my arm. My head is in his lap. He pauses and begins his reading again. I breathe in his smell. His fingers are like a trickle of water on my skin.

He stops reading.

'I'd really like to make love to you this afternoon.'

I raise my head and consider him, grave.

'Me too.'

And we smile at the impossibility of it all. Max shares a cabin with one person and I share with two. The only place we can be by ourselves for any length of time is outside. In an average temperature of −20°C that buries our bodies under six layers of clothing that can't be taken off.

'Ah, shipboard life,' Max says.

SHIVER

As the ship breaks through the ice the scraping against the hull sounds at times like fingernails down a blackboard. In the background often now, in the ship's shuddering progress, is the ice's shriek.

In the long, slow line at dinner time Max tells me casually that Jack's allowing us to have their cabin until nine-thirty that evening, two hours to the dot, to finish the final chapters of *The Little Prince*.

And so it begins.

SIX

THE DESIRE FOR BLIZZARDS AND BOGS

The ship's bogged by the white that's closing in around it. We're wedged tight by the pressure as the hull tries to squeeze between floes. The floes can't move to allow the ship's progress because they, too, are jammed tight by the push of the ice mosaic around them. At the wheel is Patrick. He can't free the ship. He calls Ivan, the Swede.

'Don't worry, Fin, the Viking's at the helm now.'

Ivan puts on his Mozart. He can't get us free either. He calls Captain Crane over the intercom. The captain steps into the room and tugs at his baseball cap and takes the wheel and after twenty minutes or so he starts what he calls the wriggle.

'I'm artificially rocking it, Fin, by moving water in the ballast tanks from one side of the hull to the other. It's on a two-and-a-half-minute cycle.

It'll cradle you to sleep if you don't watch it. How've you been sleeping. Okay?'

I smile and nod. My arms wrap around my body. I feel wet. I feel delicious. I feel loved. No-one knows, but Max and I and Blanca and Jack. Andrea suspects.

The rocking wets the outside skin of steel and in the long afternoon the ship wriggles backwards and free, like a puppy from a cat door that's too small for it.

We go slowly back into the rubbled path of churned-up ice chunks behind us and then accelerate forward fast and the ship rears up on top of the reluctant ice wedge and splits it and slides to a halt again. In five hours the ship's gained several metres. It reverses and accelerates forward, again and again.

The focus of a surgeon in an operating theatre is on Captain Crane's face. It's like sailing through sand.

As we lie cocooned under blankets in his narrow bunk like two naughty children, Max asks me if I'm in another relationship. It's taken him a while to ask. Antarctica's like that, the rules are different because you're so removed from everything that binds you in the real world. I tell Max I'm not in a relationship. I ask him if he is. He says no. I tell him I'd guessed that because if he was in a relationship, then I wouldn't be doing what I'm doing.

'Why?'

'It's just something I don't do, because I've had it done to me. This guy, he was my lawyer, he was twenty years older than me. He's a lion of a man, with an enormous sexual appetite. And then one day he just started taking someone else to the opera. His personal assistant. She used to book our tickets and suddenly *she* ended up with the seat instead of me. It was awful, *and* she was three years younger than me.'

Max starts laughing.

'I'm serious! After it was all over I said to myself I'd never do that to another woman. It's just too terrible, the hurt.'

Max listens with his chin back and his eyelids half closed. There's a long pause. A smile comes into his eyes. He lifts the blankets and takes a long look at me naked. His finger traces my nipple.

'If I *was* in another relationship, sweet Fin, would you maybe have taken off your clothes and just fallen to sleep beside me? Nothing else?'

135

I look at his ready cock.

'Yeees. But, well, I mightn't have been able to restrain myself.'

In the days of thick ice I wrap myself in his disciplined rockclimber's body. I hold onto the strength in his vividly veined forearms when he's deep inside me. Our bodies are always wedged tight together in crammed places. His fingers spread tenderly as he cradles my head like a baby's so I don't thud my crown against the close walls encasing us. Our cramped domains: his top bunk above Jack's, with my feet flat and strong on the ceiling; his narrow, boy-grotty shower, with my chest and palms flat to the shower wall and his belly to my back; and the sliver of floor between the two couches in his cabin, with a foot high on each seat.

He holds his hand to my mouth to catch my coming and giggles urgently to me, you must be quiet, you must be quiet.

The voyage's deputy leader is in the cabin next door. He's a pinched man of cryptic crosswords and gossip. No-one must know. Max checks his watch. We shower. We fuck. I check my watch. We turn off the water. Max bends and with a towel dries me softly between my thighs. He dries my feet and between my toes. I kiss the strong hills of his spine.

The phone rings. Jack wants his cabin back.

I knock on Tyrel's door and it opens curtly. He looks at me with surprise. I'm here because Max tells me I have to get it off my chest. In a rush I tell Tyrel that the snow petrel has been weighing on my mind and how upset I've been and that I can't stop thinking about it and I just want to find out why he did it. That's all.

Tyrel asks me into his cabin. I sit on the very edge of his bed. I notice whisky bottles and about twenty neat pairs of red socks hanging to dry on the back of a couch.

He sits at his desk and tells me that he loves animals much more than humans. He tells me that this is his eighth trip to Antarctica and even though he goes down to supervise the unloading of cargo it's his passion for the wildlife that keeps him coming back. That's the reason he paces the decks and stares at the sea and the sky. He tells me that he saw me day after day with a bird on the ground that should've been in the sky. He tells me that the bird wouldn't have lived stuck in a box on the deck and it kept nagging and nagging him. He tells me that during the barbecue he'd sat in his cabin and had one too many Scotches and he'd gone up on deck to free the bird because he couldn't stand it anymore.

'I honestly thought it was the most humane thing to do.'

I'm silent. Then I look at him. 'Maybe it was. I don't know. It just gave me a hell of a shock. I couldn't speak to you I was so stunned.'

Tyrel tells me he couldn't explain because he's not very good at speaking. He says Antarctica teaches you to speak out and say what's on your mind but he's never quite got the hang of it. He apologises, sternly, about doing what he did to Fin-tu and I realise then that his sternness is like the crust of a pie, that there's something churned up and confused and soft and hurting inside. Maybe Max was right, maybe Tyrel isn't so bad. I see good everywhere now, in my big balloon joy.

He pushes me out the door.

The ship's parked each night in the ice. It stops as darkness drops. There's a minefield of bergs and pack ice in the big black around us. The engines are killed and the searchlights stay on; the bridge is in darkness, illuminated only by the bright screens and switches on the control panel. Max and I stand side by side in the gloomy far corners of the room. We stare at the snow darting through the two white highways of searchlight ahead of us and the sides of our bodies furtively touch.

I feel love spreading through my body like ink pluming into water. The certainty of it pushes the panic of alone from my sleep. I bask in its rescue. I feel a serenity through me, I feel taller in my walk of the ship.

When people are around us our talk is publicly loud and when they move on our conversation drops privately low. Sleeping a whole night together is out of the question. There are public goodnights in the corridor, nonchalant see yas, and then we're off to our separate beds.

I'm up early, often, filing my stories. My concentration's ragged. I don't care. I'm deliciously distracted. I'm letting go of work a little. It's healthy.

Daylight comes weakly and every morning Captain Crane climbs into his freezer suit. With binoculars strung around his neck he climbs the mast to plot the path through the thick ice ahead. If he can't see well enough from his perch, he orders the chopper up. He takes me with him. For half an hour we sit in the chopper on the helideck while the engineers blow hot air through giant blow heaters at the engines to warm the oil. Then swiftly we're winging high. The ship below becomes an orange toy in the vast white bathtub around it and then it's gone. With a pad of graph paper and a pencil in his hand, Captain Crane draws the course that the ship will take. Humble hand-drawn crosses and lines chart our path.

'We have to be quick. In a couple of hours the ice will have changed completely.'

Below are fields of floes. From the air, the squares of ice have the neatness of cultivated country. I'm so excited at seeing my first iceberg from above I forget to take a photo. The deep fissures in the top of it make it look like a cake that has cracked as it's been taken from its tin. Captain Crane yells I'll have to find a new word for wow. He's hearing it too much.

At the end of the flight my camera's untouched. Max laughs at my crossness. He tells me that sometimes people with cameras in front of their eyes don't see very far and he says look at Jim. He points out the obedient line of icicles frozen the length of a ladder rung beside us. He says Jim would never see them. I wouldn't know.

We pass each other in the corridor now without a word.

Max and I go often to the bow. It's like a spy movie—we can talk up there in the open certain that we're not going to be overheard. It takes him nine minutes to change into his outside gear and it takes me sixteen. We meet at the end of the corridor and step into the metre-wide gap between two watertight doors to the deck outside, and kiss, and step into the punch of the cold on our faces.

'I love the bow, Finny. It's one of my favourite places on the ship.'

Max goes there early in the morning and late at night, under auroras and satellites and stars. He goes there when parties bellow on oblivious in the belly of the ship.

He tells me he hates that scene because it's so blokey. He tells me he's shy in crowds. He's thirty-eight and he says he doesn't need it. I tell him I wish I had that courage but I don't.

'You've got to learn to say no. It's a wonderful freedom.'

He tells me he's reached a point in his life where he wants to say no to a lot of things, and Antarctica's giving him the courage to do that. He says his life's galloping towards forty and he doesn't really want to go back to his job and his city and his house. He says God knows what's ahead, but he's excited about it, whatever it is.

Our bodies lean and touch.

The weather closes in as the ship sails deeper south. Steve's mop freezes to the floor of the hangar. Callie returns from outside with her hair snap-frozen. Captain Crane's shower stops when he's in the middle of washing his hair—the water's frozen in the pipes during its long journey from the bowels of the ship to the uppermost deck. Doctor Helen circulates with a new warning: exposed flesh will freeze in a minute outside.

For Max and me the mornings drag when we meet in the mess or the corridors and don't talk and don't touch because there are always other people around us and for both of us there's the strain of can't.

We come together in a rush of relief in the early afternoons. Max waits with a book in his hand on the couch by his open door. It's our neat pretext to the rest of the ship. We're the readers, reading. I come in and shut the wide door.

'How much time?'

'Till four-thirty.'

Or three or two or five, whatever Jack's allowed us.

I'm twenty-six. I've had seven lovers in my life. I've never had an orgasm. I never thought I would. Max gives me my first.

'So sad, so sad.'

It's our refrain as the ship shudders and scrapes to Mawson Station where Max will leave me. He'll be tagging, counting, photographing and recording the seals and in his spare time he'll be walking the hills and combing the old station buildings. He's never seen them, of course, but he's passionate about historical architecture. He tells me it'll be like playing in history. He wants me there with him.

'So little time. So sad.'

He'll travel in a chopper to Davis Station after Mawson. He's scheduled to arrive a day after I depart from it.

I pass Jack in the corridor as I leave his cabin and he returns to it. I say thank you, quietly, for everything. He says yes, it's a difficult situation and moves swiftly away. He's Max's best mate. I want to crack his code. Get to know him.

Wind comes. It streaks aross the ice around us, kicking up snow and making it look like fast mist or dry ice. The flung snow obscures the bases of the distant icebergs. They look like they're hovering in mist.

'Scott's party is snap-frozen in an iceberg somewhere soon,' says Mark. 'The ice chunk they're buried in is due to break from the continent around now, Fin. Calving, it's called. The iceberg will calve. I love that term. Scott, Wilson and Bowers. They're preserved perfectly in the ice. What a way to go.'

Mark's been listening intently to the talk of people around him. He stands quietly on the bridge with Max and me and shares his wonder with us.

'I love Mark's curiosity, it's so refreshing.' Max laughs savagely and annoyed at the expeditioners who spend most of their time in the video lounge.

'Some of them haven't seen daylight since we left Hobart. They live in a world of virtual darkness. Maybe no-one has told them they're going down in summer and they're acclimatising themselves to the twenty-four hour darkness of winter. They put on a comedy about nuns on a Sunday morning and that's their church service.'

Max has lost his faith. It went years ago. He's embarrassed about his privileged Anglican school education. He lets slips a childhood of Sunday school and church fellowships and still devout parents. He tells me he doesn't believe in it all. 'I'm a scientist. I can't.' I tell him that I have a belief and he says he envies me. He says my belief will give me strength to get through very rough times and I'm lucky to have it. He says he feels so alive in all of this experience, that if he did believe, he reckons this'd be as close to God as he could get.

'I look at the videoheads and they're like icebergs, all under the surface. They're not alive in this at all. They're people without curiosity. They can't be bothered going out on deck to look at whales and auroras. *Why* are they here?'

There's a button on the control panel of the bridge. It's marked X. Underneath it is a small, official looking plaque. It says in bold script, *Only to be pressed in extreme emergencies*. Max presses it.

'Fin, I have to.'
It dims the lights.

•

Jack posts a new rule for seal captures. Only male seals. They're tougher, and they won't be pregnant.

A grey slug of a seal is spotted in the distance. The ship is turned in a tight circle and slid up gently to the floe. Jack and Max and Meg confer on the bridge with binoculars. The seal's a male. It's on. Patrick puts the call over the intercom for gladiators to assemble on deck. I'm going down too: I need some more recordings. I'm in the third cage over the side, with Helen. The steel of our cage thuds onto the snow just as the gladiators throw the net. The animal slips through. It's a mighty old bull, magnificent and battle scarred and thick. Max throws himself on top of him with the net and the other men fall in after him. They're pushed off by the animal's powerful back and tail but Max and Gino have him around the neck and the other men fall in again and they've got him down. The animal's mouth stains the white net red, he's got his teeth in it, he's caught and sawing at it and gagging and trying to bark. Meg rushes in with the needle. Her face is tight and white. She's giving him a big dose. The animal falls quickly under.

He doesn't come up.

The gladiators step back. No-one does anything for what seems like a very long time. The expeditioners lining the bow are silent above us. Max is still. His face is pale and set. I can't go up to him. I want to so much. Jack has an arm around Meg. The crane on the deck drops a limp net over to us to bring the seal on board. I feel very, very tired.

There's a postmortem. The prognosis: trauma, again.

The ethics committee in Australia decides that the captures can continue. The gladiators meet to put the project's continuation to a vote. The project's stopped. The ship's drained. Jack speaks to the crowded rec room in a voice without colour or variation or volume. He says the project will be postponed. That they'll try again next year, using tranquillisers fired from dart guns. He takes no questions and leaves quickly afterwards.

I walk away from the room with a deep, familiar adrenalin rush. I've got a scoop. It'll be picked up nationwide. Fantastic audio. A great story. Award-winning stuff.

'Fuck, Fin. Fuck. Do you have to?' Max turns away from me. 'There were grown men crying in that gladiators' meeting. This has taken a terrible toll. The greenies will be onto us and the animal liberationists. Oh God. They won't understand. Fuck. Fuck fuck fuck. *Why* are you a journalist?'

He buries his head in his hands. 'This whole thing means so much to Jack, don't you understand that? It's such an important project. It can't afford to be jeopardised.'

There's a sudden ferocious anger in Max that I haven't seen before. It's quick and savage and tight and it makes me speak very calmly and very controlled in response.

'Max, it's my job. If I don't do the story someone in Australia will get onto it and then there'll be questions asked about why the journo on the ship didn't file. It's what I was put on this ship to do. I have to do it.'

I want to do it. I walk out without a word and shut his door carefully behind me and go back to my cabin and take out my notepad and start filing the stories. I write quickly, summing the situation up in thirty-second reports for the news bulletins, elaborating in four-minute items for the current affairs programs. I can feel my old self coming back, the journo in me firing. I file to the studio technicians and I speak to the editors about ways they can continue the story and I have a break and then the phone starts ringing on the ship. I'm hounded across the nation by producers and newspapers and presenters wanting followups and more information and interviews with Jack. It finally dies down and I return to my bed, high with it all.

There's a knock on my cabin door. It's Jack, telling me Max wants to see me in his cabin. I can't read Jack's face. I brace myself. I walk into our familiar domain with my belly feeling as though it's twisted into a knot and Max takes me softly and humbly in his arms and says that he's sorry he's sorry he's sorry. The knot drains from me and I flop back on the couch and he falls on top of me.

Max tells me he's heard that I've filed sympathetic and accurate stories and he tells me that Jack's pleased with the coverage and the greenies aren't jumping and he's sorry for swearing and for the anger that I saw.

'I've got a terrible temper. But the one good thing about it is that it always disappears very quickly.'

We fuck, rough and hard, and after it we lie still and drained in the sanctuary of each other's arms. I stroke and smell his soft sweet skin and smile to myself.

The phone rings. It's Blanca. The radio room's looking for me. Another current affairs show. A request for an extended, six-minute package and it's only after several hours, when I've finished it all and am standing trembling with tension and tiredness on the bridge with Captain Crane and Ivan and Patrick, that I realise I smell of Max. I smell of sex. I wonder if the other men can pick that up. I guess they can.

Jack's getting tetchy. He wants his room back. I tell Max how I thought, for ages and ages, that they were gay. He tells me a lot of people think that, that it's just the way of their friendship. He says they've known each other since uni, that Jack's shy and they're opposites but it works. He says the two of them have a mateship that's very un-Australian, with none of the macho bullshit. I say it seems more like a friendship between women and he says yeah, it is, it's good. His hand trickles between my legs. The phone rings. Our time's up.

We roam the ship searching for places to be alone. The books in our hands are our armour against curiosity. We develop a public privateness. Our fingers knot in a nest of woollen jumper as we lean towards the windows on the bridge; our elbows touch at a communal bookreading in William's cabin; we run fingers strongly down a spine in a recently emptied stairwell. Our time's running out. Soon Max will leave me for Mawson Station and I'll be sailing on to Davis. We grow bolder: kiss in corridors and risk a door opening or someone walking by. Kiss in stairwells. Entwine our ankles on the bridge.

Jack's getting tetchier. Reducing our time alone in his cabin.

We make the move into my cabin in the certainty of the lunch hours. We hide giggly and sweaty under the doona when the door is opened and Blanca or Andrea comes inside and we thread our bodies tight together, legs under legs, sculpting the shape of one sleeping mound until they're gone.

'You must be quiet, you must be quiet.'

His tongue and a whisper like a soft moth in my ear.

When he comes to my bunk from outdoors his earlobes are soaked in chill. It's as if they don't belong to the rest of him and I warm them with breath and kiss. He holds my toes in the wet cave of his mouth.

The ship seems to stew in silliness around us as we head further west. The closest country's now South Africa. Australian time is five hours ahead of us and Gino dubs Greenwich Mean Time Greenwich Really Nasty Time. Sixty-two people are crammed into a cabin. It's a record. Expeditioners consume more food now than they did before Macquarie Island when there were twenty-five more people on board.

'It's boredom,' says Henry. 'And no-one's seasick anymore.'

Mawson's only a couple of days away. People begin to appear promptly at breakfast as if they're bored with sleep too. There are fresh shirts and trimmed beards and shaved skin. I sense a relief at the coming of routine again.

Max and I, alone in it all, want bogs and blizzards to slow the ship down. The days are slipping away and there's a panic in our coming together. We grab, ferociously, the little time we've got.

The hull can only crack its way to within sixty kilometres of Mawson Station. It grinds to a halt in dazzling white ice that's metres thick. A message

comes bluntly over the intercom. Essential personnel only are to be choppered across to the station.
At first light.

Max asks me to ask Blanca if he can sleep in
our cabin on the final night.

'I couldn't ask Jack. He'd never forgive me.'

I hate the asking. I try to pick the right
moment. I finally dive into it as time speeds away
to bedtime.

'Of *course* he can, darling.'

Blanca slaps me on the bottom. She'll be sleeping right beside us.

Max and I, naked in our doona cave, fuck
grave and quiet with my back rammed to his belly.
One of his hands traps the cries in my mouth and
his other's firm and guiding over my pubic hair. We
hardly move.

Blanca's still and asleep, we hope, less than a
metre from us. We've promised not to do anything,
just hold and sleep. I'm almost under and then
there's a whisper, very close, I love you, and I smile
warm and snug and sleep tightly by him and wake
to his eyes watching mine. There's a vast tenderness
in them.

'There's so much trust in your sleeping, Fin. I
never want to hurt that,' he whispers.

I grab at his smell in the shower and I drink from the ribbon of water falling from his earlobe and drink from the pool in the hollow of his shoulder and just as he's about to slide deep inside me there's a knock. It's Blanca. She wants the toilet.

We groan softly and laugh and yell just a minute! and Max says close to my ear that next time we'll have to try an all-girls youth hostel because anything will be easier than all of this.

'I don't do this lightly,' I say in the last swift drying.

'Me neither.'

And we smile, wisely, at each other.

On the edge of the helideck there's a public, final farewell for the Mawson group. I say goodbye to Callie with a long hug. And to Mark. He gives me a jar of melting ice and his address written neatly on a chocolate bar wrapper. Meg touches me on the shoulder and grins. Gino tells me to remember to wash my hands with olive oil and sugar if they ever get too dirty. Jack just smiles. I turn to Max. We touch swiftly and gently, cheek to cheek, among the people. Our skin feels like plastic as we come together.

Max waves and blows kisses from the chopper as it shrinks into the sky, and then it's gone.

The other expeditioners go quickly below. I'm alone on the deck.

I put my face to the cold wire of the fence. I have a certainty about Max. I know the rightness of it. My mother would tell me that nothing's certain, that I'm blinded and that it's too soon. But I know the rarity of it, its anchoring power. I know in the shudder that begins between my legs and travels through my bowels and up to my breasts. It hurts as I think of him.

Cold slices like glass into my cheeks and I want to get out of it before it kills the skin on my face because that's what frostbite does, deadens flesh. My cheeks are always the first part of me to be defeated by the cold. It's −55°C, with the windchill factor. Helen is warning us that exposed flesh will freeze in sixty seconds on deck. I'm on deck. For field training. In case we ever get caught in a blizzard on the continent. It's as though we're in a milk vat of snow.

For two days and two nights the wind has been screaming through the rigging in gusts of one hundred and fifty kilometres an hour. The ship is wedged still and tight in a base of ice. We can't sail because we can't see ahead. There is a slight lull in the blizzard and it's bitingly cold and ten of us are on the snow-saturated helideck. We're sitting in a line. William's between my spread legs, his back to me, and my arms are tight around his waist. Andrea's arms are tight around my waist and her head is sheltered in my neck. It's called a penguin huddle. It's a survival strategy. I'm getting colder sooner than anyone else. I always do. I have to go inside, the chill is pushing into my cheeks and I don't want my flesh to die. I can't go inside, I can't make it across the deck by myself. I'll be blown away. I'll have to crawl. I don't have the courage to break from the huddle. I can't let the team down. The wind speed drops. I leave a gap in the line as I climb from the legs and the arms wedging me tight. My body is butted sideways but I make it across the deck in a crouching crablike scuttle. I've let the team down but I had to get inside, I didn't want my skin to die.

I know now why they put small build, question mark on my medical form. I wish it was Max between my legs. My thighs tremble, thinking of him.

That night I stand on the bridge with Ivan and Patrick and William. We stare behind the ship. It looks like the gates of hell. Snow flurries furiously in the orange reflection of the hull in the lights, as if we're in the middle of a great burning furnace of ice.

Max speaks to me via email from Mawson. He hasn't been able to begin his seal work. The weather's conspired against him. He says the station buildings are ugly and nothing to write home about. He says he, too, is trapped in a blizzard.

Looking out from the living quarters it's like being in a fishbowl or submerged in a spa. I've got a blizzard within me too. I watched you sleeping that final night, your head on my arm, and I felt completely overwhelmed. I'm in trauma, Fin. Like a seal dive response. Will I come out alive/ unscathed/intact/a more loved person? Definitely the latter. Someone touched me in a most dramatic way and that was you.

Max's words buoy my days. Blanca sits on her bunk and reads my face as I read his emails that are slipped under the cabin door by Paul, the communications officer. He prints them out for me and I trust he's keeping our secret. Sometimes the emails come in several times a day. Blanca chuckles and claps as I surface from reading them.

'Oh darling, you are gone, you are gone.'

In the days after Max's departure I sweat the smell of his skin and our sex from my pores as I work out in the gym. At night I breathe into the pillow and sheets that have soaked his smell into them. I want to roll in his smell like a dog.

'Ask her what colour they are!'

Jim's yell soars across the mess as a plumber leaves to take a phone call from his wife. It's just been announced over the intercom.

'Just for you, Stiff,' the plumber yells back.

I ask Tyrel what they're referring to. He tells me, tightly, that they're talking about the wife's underpants and he says he wishes I'd stop asking stupid questions about stupid things. (*What* is his problem?)

I email Max. He tells me that Tyrel was in Antarctica a year, the first time he was sent down, to look after the supplies and equipment. He tells me that before he went he organised a single red rose to be delivered to his wife back at home. It arrived every Friday that he was away. It cost him a fortune and his wife ran off with the man who delivered the roses. And Tyrel doesn't talk about it. Ever.

I was going to get married once. It ground to a halt in the weeks before the wedding. He was a man who was never quite comfortable with the worker and the money-earner in me. So I modified myself, reduced myself for him. I said to my mother, in the rubble after it all, that I'd never love anyone so deeply again. My mother smiled and said I would and it'd be richer and deeper and stronger and I'd thought at the time, oh yeah, what does she know.

Mum was right.

The luxury of Max cushions my days. I feel a strange calm. It settles over me like a great warmth.

SEVEN

LEGOLAND

An Antarctic map a metre wide is spread under glass on a table on the bridge. There are no lines in some coastal areas. Just dashes, or blanks next to the confidence of the blue lines that detail the known edge of the continent. The mapmakers still don't know where ocean ends and land begins under some of the great tongues of ice that push out into the sea. The glaciers thwart them still.

Our ship approaches.

William's seated beside me. His fingers tap on the chair arm. As we get closer the ship's bridge is his auditorium. There's the concentration of an audience thickly about him as he sits high up in the birdwatching chair. He quotes Coleridge, quietly, as the ship breaks through the last of the tough ice to the coast.

"'The ice was here the ice was there the ice

was all around, it cracked and growled and roared and howled like noises in a swound.'"

The ice against the hull obliges. We laugh.

William's wanted to get to Antarctica since he was a child. He carries with him a folded map of the continent. It's thinly worn in the grooves of its folds. William's had the map since he was ten. It's got a lot more blank spaces on it than the map on the bridge. He's applied for the longest stint possible—eighteen months. It has taken him six attempts to get the snow petrel job. As he sits, leaning forward, his fingers tap and tap and tap as if he's sending a morse code message.

I feel alive. New. I feel as though layers have been peeled from my skin and eyes and mind. I feel as nervy as a schoolkid in a T-shirt in winter before the big race at an athletics carnival. I'm buzzy and heady with it and I want to get out of the ship's small spaces and onto the land as soon as possible. William too.

The ship sails up to Davis Station through an avenue of icebergs. There are five hundred or more of them. They shine like white plastic in the hurting light.

I'm on the bow. Blanca comes up behind me and puts her arms around my waist like a lover. My stomach dips.

She points to the penguins fanning away on the ice from the ship's slice. They waddle like fast metronomes in their panic. Then they flop to their bellies and slide, flipper-propelled, on the smoothness.

'They're like, what you call, surf boys paddling out to a wave!'

I laugh but say nothing. I want Max with me in all of this. There are shouts from several people at the tip of the bow.

'There she is!'

And there far away ahead of us are low and sensual hills of snow. They're peppered by black rock. Landfall, at last.

In the draining light the ship batters reluctantly at the toughest of the ice. A ragged Australian flag journeys slowly up the mast and in a canny response, two long paths of brightness reach out to it from searchlights somewhere on the coast. Something stirs within us, belly deep. It's been six weeks since we've seen land. For most of the crowd on the bow, this is the first time to Antarctica. The darkness grows dense. A bunched dotting of lights comes on from buildings in the low hills ahead.

'There are so many!' William says, his voice sagging. I can hear the disappointment. He wants the frontier.

The ship slides to a halt several kilometres from the station. William comes up and kisses Blanca and me on the cheek; there are tears and hugs and cameras and kisses all around us. I want Max beside me. I want a public kiss. I reckon it'd be allowable in all this thick emotion of—finally—Antarctica.

Max is two hundred and fifty kilometres away. The only way he can get to me is a five-hour chopper ride. And he'd need a bloody good reason. I go down below to email him. The computer room's empty and I bang out words swiftly to him.

'Are you fucking him?'

It's Jim. His voice is behind me. Scrunched over the computer, I hadn't heard him. I turn, caught out, furious, flushed.

'Jim, this is none of your business, mate.'

''Course it is, it's ship business.'

He gets his computer disk slowly out of his pencil case.

'Haven't you been a busy little girl.' He smiles.

'Be careful you don't get yourself into trouble, Miss Lois, that's all I'm gonna say.'

'Jim, this is something private between Max and me, okay?'

'You do know his situation back in the real world, don't you?'

'*Yes*. I do.'

I turn back to the computer and save the document and send it into cyberspace and step swiftly past Jim's smirk. I don't know Max's situation in the real world. Not really.

As I walk fast past the rec room several people file out of it. Pumping from the flickering gloom is swelling music over the end credits of a film.

'We there yet?' someone asks.

They've all missed the Davis arrival. The bergs, the sunset, the flag, the tears. Another group's in the mess, deep in a game of poker. Tyrel's playing patience by himself in a corner. He looks up; he doesn't smile. I go back outside.

The enormity of the ship has been stopped, obediently, by a meek line of forty-four gallon drums. Five of them. They're lined up three kilometres from the shore. The hull can't come in closer because it's too shallow and too rocky ahead. A work crew from Davis has bulldozed a two-lane highway on the smooth ocean surface from the drums to the station.

'The ice is three metres thick,' says Steve beside me. 'It'll support a small truck.'

'Can I walk in tonight?'

'No fear. The light's dropped too much. You'll just have to be patient.'

'Fuck patience. I don't have much time.'

I'm rattled. I can't stop thinking about what Jim said. One of the choppers arcs away in the sky. It rudely thuds above us then sweeps low beside us.

'Showoffs!' yells Steve to the sky. 'The chopper's full of goodies, Fin. It's going on ahead to give the winterers time to read all about home before you lot invade. That's when the madness begins. The morning, mate, the morning. Just you wait.'

I range the bow like a dog in a cage, pacing and stopping and starting again. I think of Max and the little I know of his world in the real world. I want to get off the ship. The still of Antarctica's vividly in the air.

•

The cabin's bright with light and tears and tension. Andrea's on her bunk. She turns from me as I walk in the door.

'What's happened?'

Andrea says nothing. Blanca shakes her head. She'll tell me later. I rummage in my drawer and find a chocolate bar. It's broken. I reach across to Andrea and offer it. She says no thank you and smiles without looking at me and exits in a rush. Blanca puts out her contraband bottle of red wine on the desk. Pours two glasses. She stands by the porthole and runs her fingers through her hair.

'That Patrick. He has dumped her. He tells her it is a shipboard romance and nothing more. He tells her to go and enjoy Antarctica.'

'Bastard.'

'Men. So, he is one of the ones with a woman every voyage. I recognised that in my one. I did not think it of Patrick. And neither did Andrea, poor darling.'

'Poor thing.'

I feel a small, mean thrill as I say it. Andrea doesn't come back. I go to bed. Panic comes into the beginning of my sleep, pushing me awake late into the night. I think of Andrea and Patrick, of Jim and Max. What do I know of Max's life? A privileged childhood, a brilliant student. A de facto relationship with a fellow biologist that split apart eight months ago. A very loved dog, a very loved garden, a half renovated house that's giving him the shits. A city he wants to get out of, a life he wants to move away from. I don't know why.

Our relationship has existed in such a strange bubble of self-containment. It's a relationship that hasn't involved family and friends and money and houses and history.

Sleep is sparse. The morning sky is a deep slate grey. Antarctica doesn't look welcoming. Andrea is asleep above me and Blanca restless beside me. I find Captain Crane on the bridge with Len, a young sailor raw to his job. He's mopping the vinyl.

'I hate it, I just want to get home.' Len's a surfer. 'It's grey and it's white and it's cold and I *hate* it.'

'But it's changing all the time!'

'Yeah Fin, it just gets colder.'

We look outside. The sky is as dark and deep and musky as a plum. It hangs low.

'Who'd want to go out in that? You'd have to have a few screws loose.'

'Well, Len, I want to go out in it.'

'Don't do it, Fin. It kills people, you know. It swallows them up and tosses them away like an umbrella on a beach. It crushes ships. It makes fingers drop off. *And* toes. Mate, I'm staying put on this ship for the whole time we're here.'

The landscape outside looks wide and silent and waiting. Small islands poke up like teepees from the smooth sheet of sea ice. Sitting serenely above the mainland hills is the polar icecap. It's the enormous sheet at the bottom of the world that curves from us to the South Pole to the opposite edge of Antarctica. It looks like it's hovering.

'A new weather forecaster arrived at Davis a couple of years back,' says Captain Crane. 'For a week he forecast low cloud to the west. It was the icecap. It took him a week to realise it. People auctioned for the right to tell him. Three slabs of beer won. The forecaster never lived it down. He never went south again.'

The Captain chuckles in his T-shirt and trackpants and baseball cap. 'As soon as the unloading's underway, I'm out of here, Fin. It's my Davis indulgence, a run on the ice. There's nowhere to do it on the ship. I'm busting for it.'

Patrick joins us, rubbing his knuckles over his

head and yawning. A message blares over the intercom, telling us there's a station briefing in the mess in twenty minutes.

Patrick says it'll be a lengthy talk on the don'ts and a very brief one on the dos. And that somewhere in there there'll be a permission to fart form. He says there's always a permission to fart form. He winks at me and says he won't be going.

I stare again at the polar icecap. It looks like some sort of encroaching force.

A new face walks into the room. There's the surprise of young plaits and grey hair. She wears what we wear. She's shorter than me. We hear a new voice. It's soft and high and clear and in the tone of it there's a warning, don't mess with me. Pamela is the Davis Station leader. I can feel the men around me hushed and staring. We, the summerers, have been told not to push too eagerly into the wintering party's small world, to stand back and give them space. We've been told the winterers will be shy and won't mix easily. Pamela stands confidently before us. She isn't betraying any curiosity at the new faces around her. She hasn't seen a new face for seven months. She moves swiftly to rules. We know who's boss.

'There's no smoking in the buildings. We've put aside an old shipping container for that. And there's to be absolutely no dropping of cigarette butts outside. Showers are limited to four minutes because the snow's so laborious to melt. And no-one, I repeat, no-one is to go beyond the station limits alone, or in a group, without permission. I authorise all expeditions and jollies, so come and see me about getting out.'

After the briefing Captain Crane introduces me to Pamela and she smiles and says quickly, oh but we don't like journos, and we all laugh. She tells me I'd better watch out because she used to be a police officer.

We're free to go ashore. Most expeditioners scatter to do a final pack. For them, Antarctica can wait. They have a year or more of it ahead of them. I don't and I'm swiftly out.

William's energy, his impatient tallness, is behind me as we step first and second down the steeply inclined gangplank. I step gingerly from the metal to the rough crunchy white as if I'm testing my toes at the edge of a swimming pool. The snow's firm beneath me. Ahead of us is a motley collection of utes, a forklift, a small truck and a high metal oblong shape on tractor treads. William says it's called a Hagglunds. There's the shock of familiarity in Commonwealth numberplates. I laugh away the offer of a lift.

'You need to be escorted!' someone yells.

No I don't. It's my first chance to be alone in a very long time and I'm seizing it. I want to walk along the ice, I want to feel it and hear it. And I want to record it.

William accepts a lift. I'm relieved. He's handed a set of headphones for the Hagglunds. He climbs up into the cabin and waves to me and I raise my thumb in reply. There's a complicity to our joy.

The bashed-at orange hull of the ship looms above me. It has been scraped to grey in strips by the protesting ice. Shavings of paint, like curls of orange rind, rest on upturned ice that has bouldered in front of the ship. I touch a vertical row of icicles, head-height, on the spine of the bow. As I walk away I step over a crack in the ice and there's a flash of deep grey sea beneath me. I head, quickly, for the bulldozed ice highway.

There's a carnival bustle on the decks as sailors prepare to unload several thousand tonnes of cargo and enough diesel to last the station a year. It's pumped to the station tanks through a thick rubber hose. Someone wolf whistles. I look up. It's Len. He's in a hardhat. I yell to him to come on down. He yells back, no way Hose-ay.

I walk over the ocean with my esky over my shoulder and my microphone in my hand. There's the sharp scrunch and squeak and crackle of my boots on the ice. The ship sounds recede. In the distance, oblivious, is a stately single file of penguins, black and white and steadily walking. They look like Italian nuns.

I catch my breath by a handmade roadsign. It's as though the sharpness of the air is sucking the energy out of me. The sign's a familiar yellow diamond with a handpainted picture of a penguin and the words NEXT TWO KILOMETRES. Thick silence presses in on my ears. I wonder what Max is doing, if he's out there somewhere in the silence too. A Hagglunds chugs towards me and toots and I wave away a lift. Jim stares at me out of the back window, smiling ironically.

Ahead is a scattered collection of brightly coloured buildings. They look like huge steel shipping containers. Legoland, it's dubbed. I walk to it, not knowing where the sea ends and the land begins beneath me.

Jim's by the door of the main building, shooting some footage with his video camera. He catches me in the frame and won't let me go.

'Stop it!' I laugh, annoyed.

As he opens the door to let me through I ask him to keep what we'd spoken about in the computer room confidential. I say please Jim, please.

'Don't worry, you can trust me.'

He looks me straight in the eyes. He doesn't smile.

Walking into the station living quarters is like walking into a small airport lounge. Don't be disappointed, my sweet.

Max's warning, via an email. A feeling of deflation settles on me like dust as I step from the exhilarating wideness of outside into the cramped cold porch of the living quarters. The air's close and stale. Around me is a jumble of wet parkas and freezer suits and boots and hats. Beyond is a room almost disappointingly plush. There aren't many people. The new faces that are here aren't welcoming. There are one or two quick shy smiles as people rush past. That's it. I've arrived. I wonder what to do.

'Feel my fingers.'

The skin on his thumb feels different. It doesn't have the bounce of fresh flesh in it. I press his skin and release my finger. The crater stays in the pad of his thumb. It doesn't fill out for a very long time. It's like an old, soft orange.

'My fingers have gone off for good, Fin. I've wrecked 'em.'

It's Dip's third trip down. The first time was when he was twenty-two. He's thirty-three but his face is young, as though the cold has snap-frozen his ageing. He's from a town in Tasmania's south. Pamela has assigned him to show me around. He's almost frighteningly beautiful. It's a beauty that warns you away.

Dip shows me the mess with its electronic board of up to the minute windspeed and temperature and humidity readings. He shows me the kitchen where the eggs are up to a year old. They're oiled, to preserve them. 'Chilli the chef has to do the old crack and smell before he puts them in an omelette.' We walk through plush carpeted corridors to the cinema and the television room. 'We get Indian news every night at 10:30, off the satellite. India's our closest country. We know a hell of a lot about the Indian perspective on cricket.' Dip shows me the battered dartboard in the bar where the weekly tournament is held with other bases around Antarctica. It's all done via radio. 'The Aussies never cheat,' he says very solemnly. 'Not like some of the others.' He shows me the surgery and the operating theatre. 'We've got a doctor but none of them nurses in tight uniforms. If we have to do an operation, the diesel mechanic and the chef and the radio technician step in to help out. They went through a two-week training course on the mainland. I tell you, they're enthusiastic. It's frightening.' We walk by rows of pictures of previous wintering teams. The photos go back to the midfifties. They're posed like school photos. Gradually, the serious, solid rows of beards are broken by a woman here and there. And men with clean-shaven skin. And silliness.

'Antarctica's not scary anymore. Those days are over. The most common thing the doctor deals with now is dental problems. Can you believe it?

Teeth are a real bugger. You've got gorgeous teeth, Fin.'

I feel sexy and playful. My time with Max has peeled away the anxiety and the loneliness that had settled over my limbs in my city existence of 3.25 a.m. alarms.

'What's your real name, Dip?'

'I'll let you in on a secret. It's Rick. But only a few people call me that. They ring the station and ask for Rick and no-one here knows who they're talking about.'

'I'll call you Dip.'

He tells me to stick by him and keep out of Pamela's hair. I ask him what it is that she doesn't want me to know.

'She just doesn't like journos.' He smiles. 'But I do.'

I bet he was very loved as a child.

I unfold like a sea anemone in the sudden solitude of my room. A space of my own for the first time in five weeks. It's a converted shipping container from the nineteen-fifties and it's dubbed a donga. It's heaven. Tense wire ropes hold it taut to the ground. There's a small square escape hatch in the roof, for anyone who gets trapped inside during a blizzard. There's a thick window above the pillow on a narrow dipping bed. The window's record-cover sized and densely scratched. The world's wide and too beautiful outside.

I spread my backpacks around the room, I gut them and spill celebratory mess in my sudden sweet alone.

Solitude like cool mud seeps through me. My toenails get cut, my clothes get thrown off, I chatter and potter and fart. It's the spillover accommodation for summerers. Winterers and essential summering personnel get carpeted rooms in the new steel living quarters with their ski resort luxury. I like the cramped history of my old donga. My fingers run along its grimy surfaces and I imagine the beards that've slept here in the past.

I'm lying naked by myself for the first time in weeks and I savour the feel of my skin against the sheets. I flip onto my belly and raise my shoulders like a seal and stretch to the window's view. Bergs, ship, sky. I drop, flip, and put my hand into the moistness between my legs. Max. I dress and walk to the communications centre and dial an extension to his room. It costs nothing. Jack answers. He says, laughing, not you again, and puts Max on.

The satellite delays his talk by an awkward second. I drink his voice like a tonic.

Max tells me he might just make it to Davis before I leave. He says the Mawson project is almost finished and they're pushing for a chopper ride earlier than scheduled. He tells me I have to try to delay the ship.

'I'll put a fork in the diesel hose.'

We chuckle.

'Just don't tell the greenies.'

He tells me about a woman called Anya, a woman who was quiet on the ship. She's blossomed at Mawson. He tells me of Anya's dancing in the bar at night, and of her flirting, and of men circling.

'She's one of those women who are down here to have a good time. She's really letting her hair down.'

He says they've become mates. He tells me about Anya's slip-on parka that she always needs help to get off, because she can't do it by herself.

'It's so funny.'

I tell Max that Jim knows about us. That he asked me if I knew about Max's situation in the real world. Max laughs and says he doesn't know what he's talking about and that Jim's jealous and to forget it.

The nag of Anya's parka comes with me to my bed, now sour with loneliness.

EIGHT

MEN

Dip's a plumber. His workshop's neatly contained within two walls and a ceiling of topless women. Topless women are on the screensaver on his computer and on the noticeboard in his room. He takes me to his bedroom as part of his guided tour. There's a rumpled boyish boarding school bed. There's a small square window in the wall behind it. Dip tells me that nitrogen's trapped between the two layers of thick glass to barricade in the heat from the building. We lean side by side at the view. Our arms touch. I draw my arm away.

'It's my million dollar view. I reckon it's the best piece of real estate in the world.'

Outside is the frozen white sea and the big bowl of blue above it. On Dip's windowsill there's a row of thin, flat shells the colour of babies. He tells me he's collected them from icebergs near the shore that have rolled.

He collects beer cans too. 'We put them on the bamboo marker poles when we go on long distance traverses, and then the radar picks them up and we can find our way back.' He collects Russian hats from the Russian base. 'They're made of bear or rabbit or something. Twenty bucks, the guys sell 'em for. I reckon they'd go for five on the streets of Moscow.'

He takes me to the science block where he shows me a deep freezer whose lid he lifts like a tomb. Inside are layers of frozen animals and faeces. They're packed to the brim and they're in clear plastic bags that crackle with cold.

'That's my snow petrel and my Adélie, and my seal poo. I pick it all up when I'm out in the field. It's all for the scientists.'

A dead smell clusters in a thick concentration around the stiff snow petrel he holds in his hand, even though the body's trapped in plastic and frozen solid. I think of the warmth and cheek and chatter of Fin-tu.

I tell Dip I want to get out, beyond the station. He says Pamela won't let me because I haven't done field training. I tell him I *have* to go beyond the station limits. He says he's open to bribes.

The tour continues. Dip puts me on the back of his quad, a four wheel drive motorbike he uses to get around the station. As he accelerates away I hold tightly to his waist and my heavy helmet click-knocks with his. There's a ridge and we go over it with another big helmet click. My grip tightens.

'This is as intimate as I've got with anyone in eighteen months, since my medical!'

Dip's yell in the wind is carried back to me. I laugh.

'I don't reckon a finger shoved up your bum is too bloody intimate', and I squeeze tighter. His laughter's flung back in my face.

When we climb off the quad he asks me if I have a boyfriend and I hesitate and tell him no. It's too complicated to explain. And it's fun mucking around with him.

He tells me there's a harem of seal cows just about to pup that he knows about, eight kilometres from the station limits.

'And there's only one thing cuter than a baby seal, Fin, and that's me covered in marmalade.'

'Wednesday nights are wank nights and blizzards are a bonus.'

It's an old Australian Antarctic saying according to Wesley, an old expeditioner with a lot of sly, quiet wisdom. He's been down south seven times before. It gives him an authority no-one can match. He can talk about the days when it was just men on the station and huskies and sleds were still used and they didn't have computers and satellite television. He says wanking's extremely important in Antarctica. He says someone's got a tape of a blizzard to play, for when things get really tough. I don't know whether to believe him.

Wesley's in his fifties. He doesn't speak much during the course of a day. He's like a careful shepherd who fences his words tightly. But in the bar, late, there's a loosening. After Dip makes a Lamborghini for both of us. It's the station specialty. There's a lot of Kahlua and powdered milk involved. I have to keep quietly diluting it. It makes me realise that my drinking situation prior to the voyage wasn't a problem at all. After several Lamborghinis, Wesley's talk skitters. He tells me he wants to stay in Antarctica for a very long time. He tells me back home his wife has just moved in with his best mate. She's taken their two youngest kids with her. He doesn't want to go home.

'What's there to go back to? You tell me.'

The bar late at night is where a lot of winterers come out of hiding after the ship's arrival. Blanca and Andrea and I are usually there. And Wesley. And Dip. Most of the ten men and three women who've wintered at Davis only slowly thread themselves among us. We hear scraps of gossip. There's one couple who's paired up. They're rarely seen. There's the physicist whose child was born six weeks after he arrived, and the first time he'll hold her is when she's a year old. And there's Wesley, but no-one talks about Wesley much. Poor bloke, they'll say and leave it at that.

He points out a ladder in Blanca's stocking that disappears under her skirt. 'Is that a stairway to heaven?'

There's a beat and Blanca's laughter screeches over the top of everyone else's. Pamela comes up to us. Asks Blanca not to laugh. Says it's irritating several other people on the station. She walks away. Our group falls silent.

'She is, what you call, the menopause.'

'Blanca darling,' I tell her, 'I think you're right. You have to laugh. I need it, it keeps me sane. I guess it just takes a little while for some of the winterers to get used to us.'

Wesley looks at us. 'It's strange to look at a new face after so long with the old faces. It's strange and it's good. You're all like big puppy dogs, you new lot. Getting under our feet.'

A grin, like a light, is switched on his set face.

A chopper lifts swiftly and arcs low to the west. Its destination: Tzen Darn, the Chinese base a hundred kilometres away. The grim delegation that's on board is made up of the pilot, station doctor, ship doctor and station leader.

'A man's gone mad,' says Dip. 'The Chinese do it grim compared to us. Their base only gets one ship a year, in January. We get five or six, from October till April. And I tell you, their station is pretty bloody basic compared to ours.'

The Chinese man sits quietly with us at lunch time. Dips tells me he's a physicist and he speaks fluent English and he'll be on the boat when it departs and he's here because he tried to kill himself. I want to interview him. It's a good story. I know Pamela won't let me. I watch him eat the lettuce that's crisp from the Davis hydroponic shed.

He eats hunched, concentrating on the fresh food before him. He looks up once and catches my eye. I smile. He smiles back. Raises a fork held oddly in his hand.

He's in the library after lunch. He's impressed with my job. He nods and smiles yes, he will talk with me. Somewhere where he can smoke. There's only one place—the special smoking container.

The room's illuminated by an icy fluorescence. It's small. The air is thick and stale. Torn plastic chairs rim the space. There are frayed and coverless magazines on a rickety coffee table. The thin carpet's pockmarked by burning butts.

I don't smoke. If I did, that container would make me quit.

The Chinese man tells me his name is Shen and he lives in Chengdu. He asks about Sydney and am I near the water and do I live in an apartment block? I ask him why he's leaving Antarctica and he says can he buy a gun in Australia, can he go into a supermarket and buy one? I tell him no. He says he's a Chinese citizen and maybe he could. I tell him I don't think so. I feel stupid. I contemplate turning off the tape-recorder and walking away. I ask him what it's like living on the Chinese base and he says it's very hard and very lonely. He takes an old coin out of his pocket. It's round with a square in the middle of it and it's very beautiful. He tells me it's five hundred years old and he gives it to me. He goes to kiss me on the cheek and his hand grazes across my breasts. I push him quickly and gently and firmly away. The door opens. Jim walks in with an unlit cigarette in his mouth. He stops, surprised. I blush and tell him I was just interviewing Shen and the interview's over and that I'm going.

That night Shen's taken under escort to the ship. Word goes round the station. He's to be looked after by the ship's doctor. I don't see him again until I'm back on board. I'm too embarrassed to ask Jim if he had anything to do with it.

Max tells me he's mesmerised by Anya's dancing.

'It's amazingly sensual. She loves being the centre of attention. Good on her. She's having a great time.'

I want him here. Away from her. I carry the mindfuck of Anya's dancing and her parka and her smile to bed with me every night. It makes me want to hurt myself and Max, it makes me want to say something stupid.

'Don't be *too* mesmerised by Anya's dancing, Maxy.'

I slip it into the next call. Living so close to other people is teaching me to speak out and get things off my chest. Max's response is swift.

'Thank goodness, Fin, I've got strong will-power. You know what I do? I distract myself by thinking about you. Your swimmer's body. Oh God, I can't describe how much, how desperately I want it.'

He tells me his Mawson project is finished and he's just waiting for the chopper out. He tells me Pamela's being difficult with the scheduling but there's a slim, slim chance that he'll be at Davis before I go.

I'm wet as I hang up.

Dip plonks down opposite me in the mess at break-fast.

'The tour is continuing. Come, I'm spiriting you away.'

I grab my tape recorder. He takes me to the big, jolly red fire station shed.

'Fire's one of the biggest dangers. We can't afford to have our shelter burn down and all our supplies destroyed. Because then we're stuffed. And bloody freezing.'

As we walk out to the shed he tells me the baby seals are looking good.

'You'll just have to make sure the pups don't suck those titties of yours.'

'Don't say things like that,' I snap. He has to be told. His words don't sit right. It's as if Dip's missed out on learning the ways of behaviour back home because of the years he's spent down south. As if he's learnt from Antarctica codes of conduct towards women from men who were pulling his leg.

'I don't like it when you say things like that, Dip.'

He laughs and pulls back, stung.

Pamela won't let me beyond the station limits because I'm the only expeditioner who hasn't undertaken the extensive and rigorous field training. So I walk the station. Its limits extend three kilometres from the buildings. I walk beyond the hum of the generator and stop and listen to the silence of the land. It's thick. I try to record it. I can't capture it.

MEN

Max emails about his walks in the hills around Mawson. I tell him to stop gloating.

Those exquisite moments of standing beneath an ice cliff. The ice feels like Waterford, smooth and diamond hard. And then to hear the wind funnelling around it, to hear the ice crack and pop and then be silent. Oh, my sweetness! Just to listen to the nothingness, punctuated by the ice splintering. The ice is alive with sound, but you have to be still to hear it.

He's finished his project. He potters and writes about the people scurrying around him.

It seems to me everyone here has to fill their lives with trivia, keeping themselves busy, never experiencing anything of this life. But then I'm feeling so alive at the moment, they probably look at me and think how unproductive, spending all that time drinking coffee and staring into space.

He says he's paring down his life to a glorious simplicity in the ice and he wants to hold onto it. He says Bruce Chatwin wrote that if the world has a future, it has an ascetic one.

I walk away from the computer thinking about scrubbing my life spare. The trouble is, where to begin?

On the mess whiteboard, a note for me, to ring Rex urgently. It's the code name we've made up for Max. I rush to the communications centre, to a soundproof booth. The chopper's locked in. He's coming several days before I depart. As he tells me I'm reminded of the girl at school with a strange disease in her ears that made her feel as light and buoyant as a feather. She'd tell me that she felt as if she always had to hold onto the doorposts to stop herself from floating away.

I'm floating with joy, my happiness is sky-high. I love this place.

Cold kicks our faces as we step outside. William, Blanca, Andrea, Wesley and I are walking into the hills. Our destination's a rarely visited, frozen lake nestled faraway within the folds of the Vestfold Hills. We're on a jolly, an expedition that's purely for fun. I carry a spare battery for the VHF radio in the breast pocket of my woollen shirt. My body heat will nurture the battery's fragile energy.

In a tall pack on Wesley's back are enough provisions for a night in the cold, even though the walk is designated as a day only. The provisions are in case we get caught out. The weather can turn quickly. Wesley knows how to build an igloo and a snow cave and he knows the signs of frostbite and fatigue. Everyone's filled out a form detailing where they're going and how they're getting there. Except me. Everyone's hung their dogtags on the hooks in the living quarters to alert the others that they're away. Except me. I'm not supposed to be with the group. They're sneaking me away.

It seems to take forever to walk free of the station, from the ugliness of fences and poles and shipping containers and pipes. Then a rise is topped and before us, a moonscape spreads wide. We walk into the broadness of it. Snow and ice ridges up and then drops beneath us. The surface is flurry soft one step and then the next step it's concrete hard and then the next, biscuit crumbly. I can feel a cramp in the side of my groin. My thighs push against the thickness of the seven layers of fabrics encasing me. We walk and walk. The cramp concentrates into a sharp, clean pain. I'm determined not to show it. I slow, runted. Wesley turns. I wave. Onward and onward we walk. Sweat slides between my breasts. I unzip my freezer suit. It's −23°C. I've overdressed. My sunglasses fog. I can't remove them completely because I'll get snowblindness. I take off my sunglasses. My eyes snap shut then open in a thin sliver. I wipe the glasses on my freezer suit sleeve. Moisture's on the lenses now and they're filmed up quickly by a thin layer of ice. I wipe them again. Put the glasses back on. *Where* is the lake? I constantly think it has to be around the next bend and it never is. One by one we stumble into the snow's unpredictability. I drop further behind. One by one the others, except for Andrea, turn and catch me up and walk behind me and gather up my slowness. I'm embarrassed. I don't want their eyes.

'No, you go ahead, I'm happy walking behind. I want to take it all in.'

I'm thirsty. The field manual tells us to melt the snow in our mouths before swallowing it or else we'll get stomach cramps and the cold will lower our body temperature. I'm in too much pain and too far behind to stoop and try it.

We get to a ridge. I climb by swinging my leg

in a stiffening arc. I wish I had a stick to grit between my teeth. Wesley turns, and waits.

'I'm coming!' I yell, grimly cheery. Determined to endure, can't show my weakness, don't want the walks to stop.

Finally, the summit's reached. I sit on a rock and a sweet, sweet relief spreads deep through my bones.

Below us is a fairytale frozen lake cradled by hills. Its perfect frozen flatness has a strange innocence. There's a rich silence in the stillness of it all and then William's voice demanding tea comes suddenly loud into the air as if it's intruding.

Wesley gets out the thermos. He scrabbles in his pack and slaps his forehead. He's left the teabags behind. The dryness of the air has made us all ferociously thirsty. We tell him we don't care. We drink the hot water and in our mouths and our throats the liquid has the thickness of taste.

I'm cold now, sitting still. Twenty minutes ago I wanted to rip away layers of my clothing, like a heat-maddened walker in a sandy desert. I zip up my freezer suit. We eat and then for a long time we sit, letting the stillness of the land seep into us, the immense calmness of it all. Wesley takes out the radio and contacts the communications centre, letting the station know the group's okay and on schedule. We pack up and head back. My leg's stiffened with the sitting. As I walk my eyes focus grimly on the footprints ahead of me. I feel a tugging in my groin. Dammit, I've got to go. I yell for everyone to hang on and Blanca comes back and says thank goodness darling. She has to go too.

We walk over a ridge. I can't find a tide crack. I peel off my clothes and crouch. I piss strong and hot like a horse. The air on my legs and my backside is savagely cold. I redress, my fingers jumbled and wrong in my rush. I kick snow over the yellow stain. Blanca says to wait, that she has to do a number two. She gets out a plastic bag with a sigh.

'Oh darling, now it won't come. I am thinking all of it too much!' she wails.

We laugh. She strains and groans and finally stands up and puts a small, neat package in her backpack.

'I do not think I will ever come back to Antarctica,' she says without smiling and walks past me.

We walk and walk. I focus on the footprints ahead of me. Voices come back at me and arms are suddenly pulling me to a tall rump of smooth snow by our side. Andrea tells me I can't go to Antarctica and not bumslide. We climb, I don't know how I do it and when we're very high I sit with my knees gathered tightly to my chest and I'm off tumbling with the rest of them. Bumslides slip into rolls, arms and legs loosen in the speed of the falling, faces thud into snow and we are rolling over and thudding and laughing and whooping and screaming and coming to a stop in a heap of wet white at the bottom. Our bodies are smeared from head to toe with snow.

We walk on. Pain screams into my buttocks. We walk and walk. Finally, finally there's a radio pole on a hill ahead of us. Almost there. On our return my teeth are clenched tightly behind my smile.

Inside my donga I sit on a low stool. I can't move my leg, can't climb into my high bed. It takes me twenty minutes to pull away my freezer suit. It smells of trapped sweat and fear.

'*Why* don't you see the doctor, Finny?'

Max's concern is clear over the phone.

'I can't. I wasn't supposed to be there. And I don't want the rest of them to think I can't do it. I don't want the doctor to ground me because that's what she'll do and then I'll miss Antarctica.'

And then he quietly tells me Pamela has cancelled his chopper flight. She's told him she can't spare the machine and he'll just have to wait. I tell him it's probably because Blanca's started laughing again and then I start crying with it all.

I put the question to Chilli the cook: what's it like going without sex for so long?

'You get used to it.'

I look sceptical.

'You do, Fin. It's different to Australia. You're not tempted by the opposite sex near as much. You're just down here with all your friends and that sort of thing doesn't enter your mind as much as it would at home. It's not like a Friday night where you go out and say 'ooh that'd be nice'. Here it's more like brother and sister.'

'But is it hard?'

'Shit, yeah. Going without sex for eighteen months is reasonably difficult, yeah. It's all a matter of not going crazy.'

The two of us are standing side by side in the kitchen, chopping fresh basil for pesto sauce. Plastic flies are stuck on the wall above us. Chilli asks me to go outside and get some lettuce for the salad.

I put on my freezer suit and walk to the hydroponics shed. Inside, trays of lush green are fed by plastic pipes and fish tank lights. Inside, I'm hit by the smell of green and wet. It's a living clammy sensuous smell and it's incredibly alien after the crisp blue Antarctic air. I walk past trays of cherry tomatoes and basil and parsley to the lettuce at the back. They have to be carried to the kitchen in an esky because their thin leaves will snap-freeze in the cold. Dip's told me they used to grow flowers on the station. He says fancy new environmental guidelines put a stop to it. Now the only plants that can be grown are those that are going to be consumed.

'We did toy with the idea of putting flower petals in the salads, but the guys thought it was just too poofy.'

Dip asks me for my beer ration. It's a slab a month for every expeditioner, courtesy of the Australian government. I hand it over with a hug, keen to make up to him. He grins and asks me for my chocolate ration too. I say no bloody way.

We get eight chocolate bars a month. And fresh bread every day. Chilli rises at four to bake it. He says the food people request most is what mum cooks. There's meat and three veg, in some combination, every lunch and dinner time. Every expeditioner takes a turn at cooking, on a rotating roster, on Sundays. It gives Chilli a day off. Wesley's specialty is toast and Vegemite. William says he'll be raiding the freezer for the prime rump steaks. Blanca is ordered to cook paella. Jim serves up field survival ration packs. There's uproar in the mess.

'Most people have learnt to just go hungry on Sundays,' says Dip, laughing. 'Most of us can afford to. We all get fat down here.'

He's not. There's a gym in another shipping container and he uses it every day. Max starts asking me about this Dip guy.

'I'm pretty sure I'm not going to like him.'

Max tells me Anya has teamed up with the chef at Mawson. He tells me he wants to drink me.

Jim corners me in the hydroponics shed. Asks me did I ask Max about what he does in the real world and says do I want to fuck. I push past him. There's a wetness to his skin and his eyes. He's been drinking.

'Come on, Fin, we're old mates,' he yells after me, and laughs. 'It was only a suggestion.'

MEN

Drunk men scare me. I can't anticipate their next move.

We swallow wind as we grip tightly to the sides of the back of the ute. The truck's travelling speedily along the ice highway to the ship. Bergs, islands and the stretch of still white are all around us. There's wide sky and air that's knife sharp. It makes me feel vividly alive.

We're heading to a penguin rookery at Gardner Island. We're dropped at the busy ship and we walk from there to the island. There's the groin ache again, but I cradle the pain in a limp. I'm with Dip and Julia and Kim, two biologists. We pass two Weddell seals. They're asleep in the sun, oblivious to the drama of spilled blood beside them. The blood's hotness has plunged it deep into the ice. The red's etched like acid until the next fall of snow. The biologists want to find out where it's from. It could be a fight or a birth. They approach the animals downwind then come in close and check eyes and tails and stomachs and flippers. A seal twists and snaps a bark of annoyance. Dip and I walk on. The biologists continue their busyness.

I limp. I concentrate on the back of Dip's neck.

His nape is so pretty and vulnerable. He turns and comes back to me and points to the island ahead of us. I don't see any penguins. Then I do. Thousands, standing black and white in the twin of their background. Dip tells me to stay quiet and low as we approach.

'They don't like anything that's taller than them.'

Then he's gone.

I sit among the penguins and they peer and inch forward with a voracious curiosity. I take my microphone out of the esky. The penguins stop. Then they inch forward again and after several minutes they begin to raucously click and hoot and cluck. They're calling for their mates. Suddenly they stop, as crisp as a choir. They stare at my microphone. I thank them. It's an exquisite recording and I've fallen in love with their trust. I chatter away to them. They stare at me and then begin their honking again loudly over me.

Dip reappears over a rise and we head back down the rocks to the sea ice. In the distance is another island. A tall cross reaches into the sky. Dip tells me it's for a man who was killed in an explosion on the station a decade ago. I remember conversation scraps. The man was extremely popular. He was about to go home. A tough season was behind them and the boat was just about to come in. There was an explosion in the power shed. That's all I know. No-one who was in Antarctica with him wants to talk about it.

The cross sticks up stark and incongruous from the wideness of the land. Its spirituality, to me, doesn't sit right. The spirituality of Antarctica is in the air and the stillness and the hum of the silence, it's deep in the land.

We continue our climb down the rocks. At the bottom Dip wordlessly takes my esky strap from my shoulder. Further on, he bends to the ground and hands me two tail feathers from a penguin. The quills are slender and snappable. I place them carefully into my top pocket, which is sewn thin and long for a walkie-talkie. It's perfect for quills. I say thank you as Dip walks away. He turns and bows.

'At your service.'

The darling, he's trying so hard. There's a big part of him that's chivalrous and old-fashioned and sweet, but he does nothing for my mind. I think about the way Antarctica throws such a variety of people together. Boffins and tradies, journos and chefs. I don't know how Dip and I would go in the real world. I can't imagine it. I get the feeling he hasn't had much physical experience with women. I kind of like the idea of that.

We drink, sitting in our socks, until late in the evening. The spirit bottles are kept on a high shelf behind the bar. Each one's boldly marked with someone's name. Pamela takes down her bottle and pours me a gin and tonic and tells me a great station leader has to be a good listener and a good mum and a good party thrower.

'My best effort was the street parade. Practically everyone was on a float. The parade wound along several streets. The spectators were a row of video cameras set up on tripods.'

She tells me the reason she doesn't like journalists is because the last one was a bastard. She says he kept on going places he wasn't meant to and I say, a little guiltily, oh no, that's terrible. She says the last straw was when she had to go and deliver an urgent letter late one night to the ship and she rode a quad out to it. When she climbed back down the gangplank the quad was gone. The journalist was roaring off in the distance and she had to walk back, at midnight, four kilometres over the sea ice.

'He was an arrogant prick.'

She looks at me.

'But I reckon you're okay.'

With soft silliness spreading through my body, I ring Max. It's late. I'm on the living quarters' phone by the pooltable and he catches instantly the frivolity around me, the looseness in my voice which I'm trying to contain.

'I hate that scene. You should see it here, the verbal diarrhoea about dicks and bums and tits. The major topic of conversation is how shitfaced everyone got the night before. Oh Fin, I find it so hard to relate to it all. Give me a good book and a sunset any time.'

'And me?'

'God yes, and you. I'm such an outsider. I always want to bend the rules. I hate the rules here. The limits on where you can go and the limits on when you can eat. I hate being told when and where I have to eat. I want to do it when I feel like it, just like I want to make love to you when and where I feel like it.'

People pass. They pat me and smile at me and want a bit of the conversation with what they think is the real world. There are yells of hello mum, and she's been a good girl, their liquor-logged voices aiming roughly at the phone.

'Go away!' I laugh and then I'm back with Max. I can hear his annoyance.

'I'm so scared of losing you, so scared of everything being lost when you get back to your world.'

His vivid honesty brings me up abrupt. There's an absolute sexiness in his want and a trembling, delicious, deep in my thighs.

I don't get to the mess until late the next morning. On the whiteboard is a note. Fin ring Rex, urgent. I rush to the soundproof booth. He's arranged it with Pamela. He's got the chopper flight. He's coming over early.

NINE

WIND WHIP

Wesley tests me on the station lingo as we sit in the bus shed by the helipad and wait for the thump of the chopper from the hills to the west. Snotsicles are threads of clear mucus suspended frozen from the nose. Fort Knox is the locked station storeroom, where grog and chocolate are kept. Chernobyl's the station incinerator. Woolworths is the building where supplies are kept. The Culture Centre is the toilets, because people read there.

The sound of the chopper thuds in the distant sky.

'What are you so excited about, Fin? Sit down. Unloading isn't that much fun.'

When Max and I make love in my grimy donga we cry out and hoot and squeal and shout. It's the first

213

time we've been able to do that. Before, Max always had to trap the sounds from my mouth in the cup of his palm. Before, we were always crammed tightly together. Before, we were always checking our watches.

'It's like switching from black and white TV to colour!' he says.

We lie, leisurely and naked, into the luxury of a long afternoon. We read bits of books to each other and I fall asleep on his arm and wake and we make love again.

We have three days before my ship departs.

'Oh, Antarctica,' he sighs.

Blisters like thin leeches run lengthways across the soles of my feet. In the greyness of dawn Max kisses my toes and gives me three pairs of socks to put over them. We go outside into the stillness to the line of vehicles and quads. They're all plugged obediently into heaters to keep the oil in their engines warm. Max takes my gloved right hand between his two mittened fat pats of hands, and massages and pulls at my thumb.

'That's your quad thumb.' He sticks it out. 'It kills, the ache in it, after you've been heading into

the wind and the cold for a while. It has to stick
out from the rest of your fingers and work hard
to keep pressure on the throttle. As soon as the
pressure's off, the quad stops. It's a safety device,
in case you fall off. Some people wrap rubber bands
around the handlebar to keep the throttle pressed
down. It can be absolute agony after a while.'

We're sneaking away to the baby seals and an
iceberg clump. We need the quads to get to them.
I've never ridden one. We've got two, thanks to
Wesley. He looks after the vehicles on the station.

'Mum's the word,' he says to us and smiles.
'*Now* I know why you were that bloody excited
about the chopper, Fin.'

Max gives me a patient quad lesson and then
we're off over the frozen ocean. I'm slow and jerky
until I get the hang of the throttle. My thumb
begins to ache. Max keeps on zooming back to me.
I accelerate over cracks in the sea ice. I become
almost airborne over one. There's a sliver of still
sea beneath me.

'Don't look down!' laughs Max, shouting back
to me.

Suddenly, we're among the captured blue. We
ride among snaking alleys of hollows and caves and
sheer walls of ice rising high. We stop the quads.

The low song of wind is ghostly and faint around us as it threads among the skyscraper ice. We remove our gloves. Hold our hands to a sheer cliff of ice. It's deeply cold and runny wet, as if the iceberg's leaking slow water from it.

I step back into a crack. It's been split by the tide beneath it. I drop with a yelp to my groin. Under the rock-solid surface is slush. My boot slurries in it. Max yanks me swiftly and cleanly from it.

'We've all done that, sweetheart.'

I laugh nervously. 'Well, I don't want to do it again.'

'You rarely do, after you've been in once.'

We shouldn't be here. It's out of bounds, even though it's common knowledge that everyone on station makes the pilgrimage to the city of ice in the frozen sea. We move on, speeding over the ocean's surface to a field hut that's perched on the lone cusp of a bay. The building's unlocked. There's no need for keys. The hut's made up of three differently sized wooden shipping containers gutted into a continuous tube. Inside there's a grubby light. It's yellow like weak tea. It comes from two small scratched never-cleaned windows. There are shelves of tinned food and jars of muesli and a pot of frozen water on the stove in readiness for the next guests. Antarctic protocol. There's a crapper. It's a round tin, a meek foot or so high. It's in a separate room like a tall cupboard, which is tacked onto the side of the hut. The door swings wide to the view.

'I reckon this is one time, Max, when we women have got it over you men.'

'Hey, we're not *always* facing backwards when we go to the toilet.'

We laugh. There's talcum powder for cleaning skin, used instead of soap and water. There's toilet paper stacked high.

'Dammit, I thought you big boofy Antarctic blokes only used snow to wipe your bums.'

'Well, my dear, snow *is* very invigorating.'

There are frivolous folding chairs. We set them up and sit with cups of tea on the rough verandah outside. There's no wind. The frozen bay spreads wide before us and we stare at the trapped bergs like silent sentinels before the broad sky. Bliss.

'Now I know why William hates coming into the station when he's out in the field. He's gone out to Hop Island, where all the snow petrels are,' I tell Max. 'He calls the station town. He says he feels instantly stressed when he rides back into it.'

'I reckon this is as close to heaven as you could get,' Max agrees.

Night, huddled on a narrow sagging bed, under three thermal sleeping bags unzipped and spread wide. The air's as cold as a tomb on our foreheads. I ask Max softly again what Jim meant about his life in the real world. He says that he's stirring the possum. All he can guess is that it's about his de facto, Margaret, who he's been with for four years.

'We separated months ago, but we'd still been seeing each other, sort of. You have to feel loved, it's so important to feel loved in this world.'

We talk tightly together, warm, belly to belly.

'I emailed Margaret about you and she emailed back and we've made the final split. I cried for a day afterwards.'

He's silent. He stares at me and smiles.

'So now it's just you and me, kiddo.'

I gather his torso, gather up his heat, into my arms.

'I want to try going into this without fear. I'm sick of fear busting up my relationships. Does that make sense, Max?'

He nods yes, yes, yes.

•

Max whispers that no animal in their world is taller than them so that's why we have to stay low. We crawl on our bellies on the wet surface of the sea ice. Our bodies snake on a pivot of our elbows as we approach the harem of seals. A new pup cuddles his mother's face with a flipper. The pup makes suckling noises like an amplified human baby. He sneezes. His black nose kisses her.

We crawl closer still. The mother's sudden searching nose veers in our direction. The pup wriggles fearlessly forward towards us in a hello. Its wet black nostrils quiver in and out, learning the newness of us. Its small body is encased in folds of luxurious pelt. It's like a human baby that's wrapped in a fur coat too big for it.

'I reckon that if I held it up by its tail, all its bones would rattle to the bottom like a bag,' I whisper.

We giggle and wriggle across the ice to another mother and pup. There's the spread of blood in a two metre circle behind the animals. The clump of the afterbirth. The sac frozen flat. The baby seal is just a day or so old and its umbilical cord is still attached, snap-frozen in a stick to its belly. The seal flops its flippers, flips over onto its back, looks at us upside down and then with a roll is onto its belly again. We laugh with the seal. Deep, soft brown eyes stare at us. They're clear with curiosity and an absolute trust. It's humbling.

The sky's a strange green-grey and it's very low. I say we'd better think about getting back to the hut. We walk to the quads past a stillbirth obscured by snow. The afterbirth and the sac are tangled among the mess the skuas have made of the body. Max kicks snow at it.

The weather's kicked up and my thumb aches as I push the quad into the wind. It's slow work getting to the hut. When we're finally there I take off my helmet and stare at the furious sky and a bit of grit comes searing into my eye. I shake my head and scream and it slithers sharply further in and I can't get it out. Max takes my face between his hands and yells hold still and he licks and licks at my eyeball until the speck is gone and I come up from it smiling and still.

We radio the communications centre. Wesley's on duty. His voice is different, clipped, as if someone else is listening to him. He tells us to stay put. A blizzard's on the way. Wind speeds of one hundred and forty kilometres an hour are forecast. We'll be fine in the hut. Stay in the hut.

'The quads,' I say.

Max says he'll go out to secure them and I say no, we'll both do it. The wind doesn't seem too bad as yet. We pile on every item of clothing we have and step outside. Wind slices into my cheeks. The wind and the snow seem to be intensifying by the minute. We get to the quads. Max is a blur of red freezer suit and then he's gone. I start pushing the quad in what I think is the direction of the hut. Whipping white's all around me. I can't see anything but snow and I yell and all that I hear is the furious whine of the wind. I leave the quad and I push my body ahead. My hands sweep before me like a blind person. I fall. I get up. I fall again. I feel utterly, utterly alone. I start crying for Max, wailing like a cat on a city street. I keep pushing my body forward. Grit in the snow is bashing into me. I can feel the wind trying to lift me. I'll have to crawl. I'm on my hands and knees. Suddenly, in front of my face, there's the bright slap of a wall. I'm at the crapper. I want to sink my belly into the ground with relief. I want to stop there and then. I feel my way to the door of the hut. Push it open.

Max isn't there.

I'll have to go out in it again. I love him, more than anything in my life I love him and he's out there somewhere and I have to go and get him. Fuck. I look for something around the hut to weigh me down and suddenly he's through the door and falling into my arms and gasping and panting and laughing with relief.

We don't do anything but sit and hold each other for a very long time and listen to the whine of wind. We stare out at the blizzard through the small window, from our bright womb of stillness and warmth inside the hut.

Jim drives the Hagglunds to collect us. The quads won't start. They ended up buried in the snow. Max and I had to wait until the wind outside was demure before we went to the quads and dug them out with our hands. Jim smiles wryly when he sees us.

'Whoever thought you two would be so pleased to see me?'

We all laugh.

'Thanks mate,' says Max.

We attach tow ropes to the quads and climb

up the tyres of the Hagglunds and haul ourselves into its cabin. Jim hands us both a set of head-phones. Over the rumble and roar of the engine he tells us that back at the station the blizzard tossed an empty shipping container as easily as a chip packet on the beach. We smile and say nothing. We can hardly see outside. The side windows of the Hagglunds are covered in ice. Max and I remove our gloves. Our two little fingers are the only things that touch.

Jim looks at us in his rear-view mirror.

'When are you two going to get married?'

We laugh. It's as if words have been sucked out of us by the blizzard.

Back at the station there are stars in the glass of the south facing windows. Small stars on the outside surfaces that flurry the view. The glass has been scoured, like the bottom of a pot, by grit in the flung snow. Close scratches brand the paintwork of vehicles along the length of their south facing panels.

Wesley plugs the quads into the heater and their oil warms and they kick over fine. Pamela says, officiously, don't ever do it again, and then takes down her bottle and pours us all a gin and tonic. We click glasses wearily and smile.

'You journos,' she says, and shakes her head. 'I bet you don't know how to build a snow cave.'

'What's that?' I ask.

'It's a survival shelter, for when you get stuck. But we don't tell the journos how to make them.' We all laugh.

The bar's buzzing with socks and wigs and dresses and skirts. It's the night before sailing and it's Jim's birthday. The party's fancy dress. Come as your favourite woman. Jim gets slabs of beer and lots of Lamborghinis and some dope someone's managed to grow secretly in a corner of the hydroponics shed. Wesley presents him, very solemnly, with a brightly wrapped tube. We all have a guess what it is. Jim rips off the paper. It's a fluoro light from the store.

'I just thought it'd make an interesting shape when it was wrapped,' says Wesley in defence, at the laughter.

Max is back in the donga and Wesley comes and sits next to me. We don't say much at first. It's our way. I stare at the Aussie blokes in their lopsided wigs and crude red lips and tall heels and dresses and I feel a sudden flooding of fondness for them. Cross-dressing's big in Antarctica. Wesley tells me that in the old days some of the blokes used to get just a bit too excited over the men in stockings. I ask him what difference women have made down here.

'Well, the blokes have got a bigger range of lipsticks to choose from now! Nah, I reckon when there are no women on the base it's a lot like a man drinking in a public bar, and then tidying himself up to drink in the lounge bar when there are women here. If there are women on the base then we have wine on the tables and the blokes will get dressed up and make a good appearance. It's good. It's more of a community than a men's camp.'

Jim comes up to us. I tell him I'll get him a drink. He says make it several. He says he's going to miss me. I tell him yeah, I'll miss him too. We don't swap addresses.

Max and I talk late and urgently into the night in our narrow bed. We're not sure if we'll be able to replicate the intensity of our time together when we're back in the real world, but we're going to try. The past is secure and known, but we have no idea what lies ahead of us.

'I want to quit my job, Fin. My heart's telling me to. And that's what Antarctica has taught me. To listen to my heart, and to take a few risks. I'm not sure what I'm going to do. I want to be less tentative about things. We're all so bloody careful.'

I tell him I don't want to leave this place. That I've got such a sense of energy and renewal from it. That it's as though life itself has been bellowed into me, as though the wind has whipped through me and blown all the stress and the staleness from me. I tell him I feel ready to begin all over again, clean. Max says yeah, he feels that way too.

'The trouble is, how to hold onto it.'

Max looks at me and says that he's bad-tempered and cynical and that I mustn't learn that from him. He says he's always been racked with doubts and worries and he doesn't want to poison me. He says there's a joy and trust and innocence in me and he never, ever wants to hurt that.

I want to have his children. I can't tell him that. My mother always tells me to play it cool. I don't want him to feel trapped. I don't even know if he wants children. He's thirty-eight and he's never been married. So much I don't know.

•

I've forgotten stars in Antarctica. Light has pushed out the darkness for most of the time. There's a vivid lingering sunset from nine at night until one in the morning, then a short stretch of never black night that lasts just two hours and softens into a sunrise at three. I've slept sparsely during my time in Antarctica and on my last night I sleep deeply for only an hour. I've become used to grabbing at sleep in snatches.

'You've got Big Eye, Fin. We all get it down here in summer,' says Wesley as he throws my bags into the ute that's taking me to the ship. 'You'll sleep well on the way back.' He smiles slowly. 'No distractions.' I tell him I'll be waiting on the dock at Hobart when his ship comes in. 'Hey, mate, thank you. I'll look forward to that.'

I say goodbye to Blanca. She's staying on at Davis and continuing to take her phytoplankton samples until the next ship. She says she'll keep an eye on Max.

'Good, good. And you must come and stay with me in Sydney. Before you go back to Spain.'

'Darling, I will. I will cook for you my paella. You will show me the boys of your city.'

'Blanca, they're all gay.'

I hug her tightly. I know I'm going to miss her

terribly on the voyage home. I also know I'll have her as a friend for life. Andrea's on a glacier, measuring the ice. She'll be returning on the next ship too. I've hardly seen her in my time in Antarctica. I tell Blanca to say goodbye to her for me. It seems limp and lame. I tell Blanca that Andrea is welcome to come and stay in Sydney too, on visits from Wollongong. She smiles and says she will tell her. William is on his island with his snow petrels. I'll say goodbye via email. Antarctica's like that: sudden vivid friendships or enmities, and sudden goodbyes. Everything's intensified by the close quarters and the long timeframe and the shared experience of the continent's strangeness.

Dip wraps me in a bear hug. I can tell he has no idea about Max and me. I tell him we should get together when he returns. I'm not sure if we will. He takes a photo of me to show his mum. He gives me one of the shells coloured like babies. I smile wide and then hug Pamela. She says she'll miss me. Jim overhears and tells me to get it on tape. I turn to him. We smack each other on the shoulders. It's an uneasy truce. He's got eleven months of Antarctica ahead of him. We'll probably never see each other again and we both know it.

I turn to Max and hold him in the frame of

my camera. It hides the sudden tears. The warm flesh of my cheek sticks to the cold metal of the camera. Quickly, I pull my skin away. I was trying to get a closeup of his eyelashes dusted with ice. It looks like white mascara.

I don't want to leave this place.

Max walks me to the gangplank. He slips into my hand a small round stone, pure white and as smooth and rounded and beautiful as a miniature Brancusi.

We hug. We don't kiss.

TEN

COMING CLEAN

After a long silence the ship's engines roar at the ice. Nothing happens. The ship's very still in its tight embrace of white. The engines sound immensely frustrated. They strain and stop and then roar, insistently, again. There's no movement. For an hour, there's no movement. We're stuck! Oh joy! Another day, maybe a week! I raise my thumb, quietly and conspiratorially, to Max on the ice. Then there's a sudden soft slide back. The hull's free. Damn it. The horn blares triumphantly. I've never liked that horn. The ship reverses slowly and Max's waving arm diminishes and he walks away and I've lost him and the ship cuts back deep into virgin ice and turns and slips away along an alley of icebergs. They shine vividly in the sun.

In an hour the continent's gone. There's just ice, and icebergs, and a very big sky.

I go below to small spaces. In the background is the continual hum of the engines. I can't find silence and the air smells plastic and wrong.

The cabin seems incomplete without Blanca and Andrea bursting into the bathroom and stepping over my legs and flopping down beside me. I longed to be alone when they were loud all around me, and now I long for their company. Everything's too neat and bare. I spill lots of mess from my bags; I rubble the antiseptic length of Blanca's empty couch.

I'm in my bed. The air trapped in the sheets is sour with fart. I hold in my hand the small, white rock. I want to cry with the leaving of it all.

The voyage home's a lot quicker. We're heading into summer so there's less ice and we're not stopping to catch seals and we're not making diversions to Mawson Station and Macquarie Island.

On the way back there are only twelve expeditioners. The ship is built for a hundred and the interior pockets us away in small places. The bridge and the rec room are spare and the bar is near silent. It's lonesome and quiet and sad.

I'm deeply tired. Big Eye is gone. I want to dive into sleep.

The ship has been transformed into a floating garbage truck. Its belly and cargo decks are filled with a year's accumulation of rubbish from Davis Station. Anything that can't be incinerated is coming back with us.

And the ship carries back Shen, the suicidal Chinese man, and a handful of winterers who are coming back early. We make a motley crew. The winterers are from several stations. They've been RTA'd—Returned To Australia—for various reasons.

'None of them good,' says Simeon, my gossip king in the bowels of the ship. 'They're like damaged goods, being returned because of fights on their station or marriage bustups back home, that kind of thing. And some people just hate it. They have to get away from it, all that white. They go stir-crazy.'

I want to interview some of the winterers but they stay in the shadows of the ship. I don't see them much at first; they're quiet and they don't seek out company. They're focused on home.

Helen gently parts my thighs and with sure hands presses the muscles around my groin. I'm naked from the waist down. She says my injury's been caused by the freezer suit crotch that came down to my knees.

'It was all the strain of your body pushing against the layers of fabric when you were walking.'

'I reckon they gave me that freezer suit deliberately, Helen. Cripple the journo! Stop her from getting out!'

We laugh. My stomach flutters as Helen's fingers press on my inner thigh. I'm starting to get turned on. I think of Max. Taking his earlobe in my lips, sucking on the softness and my tongue playful with his loop of gold. Wrapping my body around the foetal curve of his back, my hand threaded under his arm and across his chest and the sweet softness of flesh to flesh.

My bashed-at body is eased onto the mattress. It's bruised and blistered and the ache runs deep, like an underground river, along the length of my arms and legs. In the long stretches of being alone I assess the battering of Antarctica: wind-scoured face, sunburnt nose, dry flaking skin, torn nails, bruised knees, lines of blisters on the bottom of my feet and two huge blisters like twin pompoms on the end of each big toe. I slice through thick skin with nail scissors and warm fluid spills across my fingers. Now there's no-one in my cabin, all my disgusting habits are coming out.

The hairs under my arms have grown. They're straight and an inch or so long. I raise my arms in front of the mirror and stare at my armpits. I've never had hair under there. I began shaving when I was twelve. My stepmother gave me a razor as a present and I thought it was immensely cool. And now, fourteen years later, I have my first underarm hair. I like it. I'm not wearing makeup or scent. I have just a few changes of clothes. Everything I need is in a pack I can carry on my back.

It's a spare life and it feels good. I want to hold onto it but I'm not sure if I can.

Emails accumulate under my door. Max's worried he'll lose me in the hugeness and the busyness of the big smoke on my return.

I feel so removed from you. It feels like worlds have been traversed but we're so far apart.

He swiftly gets a return email: he's not going to lose me.

Blanca emails. She's found a lover. 'Corgi'. A carpenter from Darwin. She says word's got around among the men in the Davis workshop, and her man 'is being get hell. They will not stop at getting him.' I laugh and laugh.

I begin emailing my family and mates back home. I tell them I've met a man. I've left the telling until now because I wanted to wait for it to move into something certain. The questions begin. How old, what does he do, how did you meet? Where does he live? Does he love books? Is he funny? Is he the one? How do you feel?

My joy feels as tall as the sky.

The question I love the most is, is he hairy? I'm not sure what they expect of these Antarctic blokes. Is it going to be disappointing if I tell them he's a clean-shaven, grey-haired thirty-eight year old who's terribly clever and loves movies and animals and cooking and joints and books? And he's gentle and funny and I love him? I tell them exactly that.

Sebastian is sitting in the birdwatching chair on the

bridge. He's been doing a stint as doctor at Mawson. I stand beside him with a set of binoculars and stare out at the white. We talk about snow petrels and the thinning ice and eating mangoes again and wearing singlets and when he's laughing I slip in that I'd like to interview him about his time on the station, and how he's changed, and how he's preparing for home.

He looks at me and says oh yeah, you're the journalist. He tells me he wouldn't be very good. He tells me to find someone else. I say okay. I'm tired of chasing interviews, of pushing myself at people.

Tyrel's in a far corner of the bridge. I didn't see him the entire time I was on the continent. He stayed on the ship, co-ordinating the cargo. When I leave the bridge, he does too. He comes up swiftly behind me in the corridor.

'I wish you'd stop being a journalist sometimes, Fin. There are some occasions when it's just not appropriate. You really piss me off at times.'

Tyrel's teeth are yellow and crooked and in my face. I bet he grew up in England.

'Sebastian's going through hell.' My face is beginning to burn. Tyrel's words trip over each other. 'He—he went down south with his wife. It was one of those rare situations when a couple can get down south together. She's a physicist. She ran off with someone else on the station and, and the three of them were stuck there over winter. For seventy-one days of darkness. Sebastian hardly said a word about it to anyone. Can you imagine the absolute agony of that? Can you?'

'Oh God, I'm sorry. But I can't help it. I don't *know* these things. No-one tells me.'

'We don't tell you, Fin, because you're a journalist. But *I'm* telling you. *Not* as a journalist.'

Tyrel's smile looks as though it's being dragged out of him. I could tell him that my whole job is about betrayal. But I don't. He says sometimes life's bloody tough. I say I know. He says he does too; he says he's been knocked down so many times he can't remember the numberplates. We suddenly, loudly, laugh and laugh.

There's brilliant blue sky and sunshine as the ship slices north. There are sun sparkles on the ice in the hurting light. Antarctica is showing off, taunting us with its splendour as we sail steadily away from it.

The ocean's crust cracks and rots. Ice thins

and loosens and becomes as fragile as sheets of glass. There are no more penguins and no more seals. Then, one day, the snow petrels go too. Wandering albatrosses replace them, circling the ship. Fin-tu seems long ago. I feel as if I've become someone else. My face in the mirror looks different. Sharper. Older.

At night darkness closes in on the voyage. It's strange to see it again after the luxury of light for so long.

Max is out in the light and the ice a lot. Just him and Jack, tagging the seals around Davis and monitoring the pupping. He writes that it's light almost all of the time, and he loves it, especially the stretched out sunsets that darken into a sunrise and then it's day and then sunset and sunrise again.

It's magnificent. I wish you were here! You know what we are, Finny? Lovers of light. There's a word for it, I found it in the Davis library. Photophiliacs. People who seek out light and the phenomena associated with it. It makes us sound like something vaguely obscene, doesn't it? I can't believe that this place of ice and snow and water is a desert. Let's get out into other deserts when we get back. More sunsets! More skies! Yes!

One morning there's a familiar creak in the wall behind my head as I wake. The ship's gently rocking from an ocean swell. It's been so long since we've felt it. Out of the porthole is the pure blue of ocean, dipping and heaving. Drops of water flash past the window. It's as though the ship's melting, its festive covering of snow slipping away.

By the afternoon I'm queasy again. Shit.

Tyrel grins as he hands over the last of his patches. Helen's told me he's the only one left on the ship with them.

'I could do a roaring trade on the black market, couldn't I?'

He brushes away my offer of money. Tells me to use the bathroom of his cabin to put it on. While I'm washing my hands he sits against the door on the other side and says that he doesn't mind if I have to do the old technicolour yawn because he can't smell it anyway. I ask him why. He tells me he lost his sense of smell in a car accident fifteen years ago. I ask him what smell he misses the most. There's a long silence. He says the smell of a woman. There's another silence. I don't say anything. He says other countries. He says he's more depressed now, generally, because of it. There's another silence. He moves away from the door.

Tyrel is at his desk, his back to me, when I step from the bathroom. He doesn't turn around when I say thank you and see ya. It hits me, as I walk out the door, that maybe there was the beginning of a love scene in there somewhere. And that Antarctica didn't have a smell. I realise I have an immense fondness for bloody stubborn strange old Tyrel.

Zero degrees. Expeditioners celebrate by wearing shorts and T-shirts. I can feel a lifting of hearts among them—an Aussie summer, its slippery sensuous air, is somewhere ahead. The expeditioners go out onto the swiftly moving deck, they hold their heads to the wind like dogs in the back of a ute.

I'm feeling weighted. Everything's drawing to a close too swiftly. Max emails and taunts me with Antarctica.

To stand or sit still without speaking and hear the low hum of being alive—it's like experiencing a taste of the infinite, a glimpse far, far beyond our frail existence. Oh Fin, where are you.

Shen starts ringing my cabin.

'Sorry, wrong number,' he stutters every time.

I wonder if he's learnt the words from Hollywood and start locking my cabin door at night. It's the first time I've locked a door during the entire trip.

The addresses of new mates are transferred from battered business cards and chocolate bar wrappers into my Filofax. The network spiderwebs across Australia and Europe.

There's a pattern of big lives, of living in remote places, of grabbing at life and not following the line of least resistance. They email me with their plans, post-Antarctica. Blanca wants to stay in Australia and open a Spanish restaurant, William is thinking of Greenland next, Callie of Tibet, Wesley of the UK, Mark of anywhere other than WA. Max tells me we should run away to the desert and write books and I tell him I let that dream fall by the wayside long ago. I tell him something that my father said to me once, about how he had dreams a long time ago, when he was nineteen or so. And then life took over.

Max emails back. His response is dismissive and optimistic. *Different generation.*

•

Emails crowd my days. They come in from people back home busy in the city. There are invitations to brunches and dinner parties and barbecues. I feel as though I'm witnessing myself becoming fashionable. The crammed life comes at me, weighing me down with its push. I don't want it. I email back to the city people and say no to most of them, tell them I need a bit of time to ease myself back into the world, and I walk away from the computer room feeling buoyant.

I go up to the tip of the bow. Wind and salt bash my face. My mind hasn't been this clear for years. Antarctica has filtered the shit. I'm coming home clean.

Max emails his approval at my refusals. *Sartre said the essential freedom is the ability to say no. Yeah.*

He tells me he's going on a four day walk, to say no to work for a little while and to soak up the experience of the land before it's too late.

I'm so looking forward to this walk. Off station, no-one else apart from Jack and he doesn't count. It'll be just the sky and the clouds and the barren rocks, the hills and valleys and deep lakes. It'll be good for my soul, Finny. I need to find a quietness of the soul.

•

Captain Crane stands at the wheel on the bridge. We watch the great dip and rise of the bow ploughing through the Great Southern Ocean. The sky's different now, more complex. Clouds shunt stately across the sky's width. They're like slow trains at a depot, some to the left and some to the right. Captain Crane tells me tales of his other travels. Of washing his plate in the sand of the Sahara, of his cottage of six windows by a Swedish lake, of his children in several countries. I begin to think of soil on my hands, sun on my back, my fingers on the belly of a cat, the taste of bananas in my mouth and the smell of horses and bushfires and grass.

The ship picks up ABC radio as it sails under South Australia. The familiar news theme slices through the chatter in the mess. The expeditioners' lunch time talk stops. There's a focused listening to the clipped, velvet tones.

The first story is the rape and murder of a nine year old girl in Perth. For me, it's too soon for all that. I don't want the newsroom just yet.

Ivan turns back to his food. He tells me he has a deal with his wife—if anything goes wrong back home, she won't tell him until he returns.

'There's nothing I can do at sea, Fin, except be frantic about it. I can't get home any quicker.'

I'd have to know.

The Australian government gets back every piece of Antarctic gear we have, except for those things that were touching our skin. We line up in the mess and I hand across balaclavas and hats and shirts and trousers and parkas and, lastly, my Honest John freezer suit. The smell of my sweat's deeply ingrained in it.

Tyrel's beside me in the queue.

'Now don't go shoplifting when you get home, Fin.'

'What do you mean?'

'Well, the expeditioners sometimes have this little problem when they return. They go into stores and take stuff off the shelves and walk out without paying. It's because they're so used to doing it in Antarctica.'

'Tyrel, I don't believe you.'

'It's true! There'll be a team of psychiatrists on the next ship out—that's when most of the winterers'll be coming home—and the psychiatrists will be easing them back into the real world. Teaching them money again, shops, keys, that kind of thing.'

I tell him thank God the psychiatrists won't be taking a look at me. We laugh. I'm excited, now, about getting back. There's an anticipation deep in my bones. I'm excited about coming home and I'm excited about holding onto the scrubbed feeling that's in me. I feel like I'll be stepping off the boat with a core of calmness. My limbs feel loose, my mind alert. I'm ready.

I climb out of sleep with the knock on the door. There's a moth-darkness that's thickly around me. Someone's calling my name. I snap out of sleep. My heart thuds with the urgency of the voice in the dark. It's Helen. I step, rumpled, into the glare of the corridor and my hand rubs at my eyes. There's a phone call. A graveness has dropped like a mask over Helen's face. The only clue I get, as she propels me to the bridge, is the gentleness in her hands.

The first thing I notice on the bridge are the very bright lights. The room never has lights on at night. Captain Crane and Ivan stand side by side and there's a knowledge in their tender glance that

I know nothing of. My fingers feel suddenly detached and light and dry as I step into the radio room and the door is shut carefully behind me and I pick up the phone with a questioning hello. There's the scratch of Antarctica in the line. It's Pamela. I ask her how she is as if I'm trying to stall something, I don't know what. She tells me she's okay. She sounds utterly drained. She tells me she has some bad news. Max is dead.

There's a strange floating feeling, a serenity and a centredness in me as she begins to tell me and then I say oh no over and over again under her words. Oh no oh no oh no in an octave lower than I've ever used before. It's like some terrible chorus. Then panic rises like bile in my throat.

Pamela tells me a blizzard blew up on Max and Jack's walk. Max had gone out to watch the sunset and when he didn't return Jack radioed the station and they had to wait for the weather to drop before they could get the choppers out. They found Max in a snow cave. He was curled up. They don't know when he died.

His body has been brought back to the station.

Pamela tells me, with great concern, to look after myself. She says to make sure people are with me. I hang up the phone very carefully.

'Max is dead.'

I can't scrub from my mind Pamela's first telling, the weight in her voice, her words.

'Max is dead.'

I don't know how I get through the long hours of night and day that follow the telling. Scraps of memory. Helen and Captain Crane's strong and calm arms getting me back to my cabin. My body thudding at walls. My face sliding down surfaces slippery with tears. My fingers tightly bunched in the hair at my temples. My wailing and wailing and saying his name over and over and wailing again. Snot-damp tear-damp sheets. Helen there, often. Saying someone has to be with me. Henry gentle with a tray of food I can't eat. My hurting head. My raw eyes, ragged with grief and disbelief.

I ring my mother and at first she doesn't know if I'm laughing or weeping and then she's weeping with me.

'Oh, my baby, my baby.'

I rush out to the deck with cries and screams for the sky to hear. I lean far over the railing and look down to the towering drop and the swell in the ocean heaves to me and I wonder where he is.

It's a while before I speak to Jack. After the search he was taken back to the station and heavily sedated.

'Do you really want to know, Fin? It's pretty awful.'

'Um, yeah. Yeah I do. I have to face it.'

I can sense him thinking where to begin.

'We were staying in a field hut. It was about ten k from the station. Right on the coast with the hills behind us. It was a really strange, sullen evening. The clouds were low, like one big blanket across the sky. The sun was sort of streaking across their underbelly.' His voice is calm and thorough as he recollects.

'The sky was just incredible. You know Max, he *had* to go out into it. He wanted me to come on a walk with him but I was really tired. So, he went by himself. He took his book, *If on a Winter's Night a Traveller*. He said that he was going out to this bluff that was sort of nearby, to watch the sunset and read. I—I dozed off. I woke with a start at eleven-thirty. Max wasn't back. The wind had kicked up. I went outside. It was really blowy. I couldn't see him anywhere. I yelled and yelled. There was snow everywhere. I started to panic. I went back to the hut and radioed the station. They

couldn't get the chopper out to us until the wind
died down. They said to stay inside no matter what,
because they didn't want two people out there and
I'd never be able to find him. So I had to sit it out.
I waited in that hut for fourteen hours for that
fucking wind to die down.'

'Oh Jack.'

'The chopper came out as soon as the weather
settled. Then the other chopper came with more
people on board. We searched for six hours. Wesley
found him. He knows the area. Max had built a
snow cave, just like the manual says, in the leeway
of the bluff. But he must have done it in a real
hurry because . . . because it had caved in. I was
digging beside Wesley. When we got to Max he was
curled up like a little kid.'

There's a pause.

'His skin was yellow. It's like he wasn't there.
His body was a shell.'

There's a stillness between us over the phone.
In Jack's careful telling it's as if he wants to get it
absolutely, utterly right for me.

'I had to tell Pamela about you two, Fin. I was
so worried about how you'd hear about it. I
couldn't tell you myself. I was a mess.'

'Hey, it's all right.'

He's lost, completely, his coldness. I can sense in it all the start of a friendship, anchored by our love of Max.

'How are you going now, Jack? Are you okay?'

'Oh, up and down.' He laughs clumsily. 'I'm just getting off the sedation now. What about you? We're all really worried about you.'

It's easier for both of us to be concerned for someone else.

Deep in the night I toss and turn, it's like my body is vomiting sleep. My mind gnaws at whatever were Max's final moments. The snow pinging into his cheeks, the scrabble to build the cave, frantic hands making blocks of ice, the crawl inside, the curling of his body to ward off the cold, the utter aloneness, the endless snowing, the scream of the wind, the checking of his watch, the hurting chill, the crack and the caving in of the blocks, his knowing.

My eyes are wide, my pillow is snot-webbed and sodden.

What he went through, I'll never know.

Another phonecall early in the morning.

I dread them now.

It's Lyn. The newsroom has just received a press release from the Antarctic Division about Max's death. She wants me to file. Expeditioner reactions, that kind of thing. My hand clamps in front of my mouth, as if it's catching at something coming up.

'We need it quick. Fin?'

'I can't do it, Lyn.' I tell her briefly that I crossed the line, I fell in love.

'Oh, God. Can the story, darling. We'll handle it from this end. Oh God, oh God.'

I sob my relief and thanks to her.

'Look after yourself, Finny. And don't hurry back to work.'

There's a sunset service for Max on Anchorage Island. It's held near the cross of the man killed a decade ago in the explosion. The Davis tradies erect another steel cross for Max. It reaches up six metres into the wide Antarctic sky. Around its base is a huddle of rocks, each one placed by a different expeditioner. As word of the relationship spreads around the station, I begin to get emails. They wish I was there. Blanca rings and says darling and cannot go on because of the sobbing from both of us. She hangs up the phone, telling me she wants me there with them. I'm ambivalent. I want to see Max. I want to say goodbye. But I feel now that I can never return to Antarctica. I just don't want to go back. His body is in a science lab on the station until his family releases it for burial in the ice. I feel so removed from it all.

I know so little of Max in the real world. His parents and brothers have never spoken to me. I ring the Antarctic Division to get their number.

The woman on the end of the line's defensive and officious.

'You do realise he was in a de facto relationship? Margaret is officially listed as his next of kin. I don't know if the family knows of you. I don't want you being difficult.'

'Oh no, of course not, of course. I realise that. I just wanted to pass on my sympathy.'

I hang up. I feel suddenly unclean. The tears come and come.

ELEVEN

TERROR

AUSTRALIS

Len says we'll get rain as we sail into Hobart. 'I'm a surfer, Fin. I can smell these things. I just know.'

We stand on the deck and smell Tasmania before we see it. Smell soil and trees on the breeze. Then see green. Hills and trees and lawns. God, it's been such a long time.

A cosmonaut who'd been in space for a year said he knew he was truly home the moment after he'd crashed in Siberia and opened the hatch and smelled the earth. I know what he means as I breathe in deeply the smell of the land. We're home.

Len was right, it's raining softly. We're the coldest we've been on the trip because we're in T-shirts and we're standing wet in the wind. Our flesh is goosebumped. It's odd to see it. I rub the wetness of the air between my fingers and shiver.

The group on the dock looks solemn and

small. My mother's standing a little to the left of it. Her stylish city-face keenly searches me out. I see her before she sees me. She looks very small and very alone and I'm suddenly crying.

Sebastian comes and stands quietly by me, a shield from the rest of the expeditioners. I feel an absolute connection as we stand side by side. I want to turn and bury my head in the warmth of his chest, but I don't.

In our Hobart hotel room my mum rubs at the crease between my eyebrows, she kneads it and kneads it as if she's trying to rub it away. I crumple and weep for the loss of the possibility of Max, for what was ahead for the two of us. Mum holds me in her arms and rocks me and rubs my back as if she's trying to draw the pain from deep in my bones. She tells me she'd do anything to take on my hurt, to spare me. On her cheeks are tears stained grey by mascara and I look at her close and realise she's always been there for me and I feel like I'm only just recognising it.

I ring my father. I ask him to come down to Hobart to see me. He says he's busy. I ask him to come and see me in Sydney when he returns. He says he's flat out with work. I tell him I need him. He tells me to get out to the lake some time and sit still for a while and look at the moon. He tells me I have to pull myself together, I have to toughen up, I have to be dignified with my grieving. He says who is this bloke anyway?

I hang up.

My period's due and it hasn't come. The stress of the morning shift has mucked it up for ages but it's never been as late as this. My mum tells me it's probably the shock. A cold's come on too. I'm all snivelly and runny from my nose, it's as if my whole body's crying.

The stern woman from the Antarctic Division rings. She tells me there's a service at the Division in three days' time. She asks if I'd like to come along. There's a pause.

'How are you coping anyway?'

'Oh, oh, I'm not too good.'

My voice wobbles out of control and there's a sudden, fierce compassion from the woman which takes me by surprise.

'I'm going to arrange a counsellor. The

Antarctic Division has a service it uses. I want you
to see someone. I think you need it.'

She gives me her home phone number and tells
me to ring any time I need to, day or night and I
hang up and there are tears in my eyes with the
kindness of it.

My mother flies, reluctantly, back to Sydney ahead
of me. I tell her I have to go to the service alone.
While I wait for it I wander the streets of the city
by myself. I feel like an alien in it. There are too
many colours and too much noise and too many
smells. The concrete pavements are too hard after
linoleum and rubber and snow for so long and I
jar my shins. Cars drive too fast. There are too
many people. Too many faces. I've forgotten
civilisation. Keys again. Money. I leave my card in
the automatic teller machine. I pick up photos and
pay for them and walk outside, leaving the prints
on the shop's counter. I'm having to think how to
function again in the world and I'm not doing very
well.

At the service Captain Crane contains my trembling

to the dark of his chest and when I weep he shields me and quietens me in his arms as though he's calming a frightened flapping bird until I've stopped.

I don't remember much about who spoke. I didn't know any of the speakers. But I remember something that was said.

'Let Max's untimely death remind us all to live our lives with his passion, and to do the things we really want to do.'

I walk up to his elderly parents at the end of the service and introduce myself and in their warm bewildered greeting I can see there's no knowledge of who I am. It's obvious Max didn't tell them. I feel in the hurt of it like a sea anemone that's been prodded by a finger, all my senses and surfaces contracting. His father knows nothing of this. He introduces me to Max's younger brother who looks mockingly, achingly like Max.

'Keith, this is um, oh dear, I've forgotten your name.'

'Fin.'

'*Fin*. That's it. She was on the boat with Max. Wasn't it lovely of her to come to the service? Thank you so much, dear.'

There's an absolute knowing in Keith's face.

'Fin. It's *so* good to meet you.'

He takes me aside. Without saying anything we hold each other very close and all my weeping spills out again and his does too and I sense that Keith's lost a part of himself and he'll never be whole again.

We go for a walk in the grounds of the Division. Keith tells me he knows all about me, but his parents don't. He tells me Margaret and Max had never told their parents they'd separated.

'The parents were the only people they hadn't yet told.'

He says there are a lot of things his parents don't know about Max, and a lot of things they will never know. He tells me Margaret has indicated that she never wants to meet me.

As I say yes, I see, I understand, I think of Browning's line: 'I listened with heart fit to break'.

'It's a very difficult situation,' says Vivien, the counsellor. 'I've never come across anything like this before. I think . . . I think you have to just let some things rest.'

'Yes.'

Tears come hotly and quickly again. So many

tears. How could I have so many in me? I apologise and Vivien says not to.

'Tears are good things, honey. They've got a natural opiate in them.'

She's gloriously, blousily hippy-herbal. I tell her about my dad. She says he obviously needs to know about the therapeutic qualities of tears and that he's a typical, older Australian male stuck in the 1950s who can't express his emotions. She says he's calcified stuck by that lake and not to take his words to heart. She says I'm doing fine. We laugh.

I tell her about the strange feeling I've been getting, in quiet moments, that Max is with me, tenderly close. I tell her about lying on my belly on a bed, and feeling him gently lie on top of me for a moment and close his eyes serenely and then be gone.

'Are you on ecstasy?'

'*What*?'

'Are you on ecstasy?' The taxi driver asks again, on the way to Hobart airport.

'No. Why?'

'It's just that whenever someone gets into my cab and they're on ecstasy, I start breathing really

deep, and with you, I don't know, I started breathing really deeply.'

I laugh softly. He doesn't get an explanation.

'Your presence is just like, wow, amazing.'

I settle back into my seat. There's a new
calmness through me. I feel older and stronger, I
feel as though something has deepened within me.
At the airport toilet I look in the toothpaste-
spattered mirror. The knot between my eyebrows
has smoothed away and the rawness in my eyes has
gone. I feel as though I'm getting my face back.

Clouds taunt me during the sunset flight home.
They look like ice as the plane skims over them. I
imagine Max's soul dipping and soaring over the
ice and rock and snow. I think of the faith that is
helping to pull me through, the belief that he's out
there, somewhere. I remember a phrase I'd heard
once: God gave us the gift of suffering. I have to
find a gift in what's happened, God knows how. I
reckon it's got something to do with finding a
quietness of the soul. And moving on in a way Max
would want me to.

But how?

I hold in my hand a small white rock. It's the
only tangible thing I have of Max. The airhostess
offers me a newspaper on a tray. I say no. I can't

bring myself to read the news just yet. The hostess' makeup is too thick on her skin. I can't see her face properly.

Mum and Simon are at the airport and they drive me to my home. There's a bone-white full moon. I lean my face outside the window and look up at it. The footpaths are buzzy and busy. It's a summer Saturday night and in the honks, and revs and shouts from the streets I feel like I'm back in the stinky belly of the city too quickly and I'm not quite ready for it yet.

In my apartment there's champagne and flowers and photos and questions. Do I still have all my fingers and toes, how cold was it, what did I eat, what did I wear, was I scared, what was it like? Tyrel told me, as we stood for the last time together on the deck, that Antarctica is like sex—it's really hard to explain it to someone who's never experienced it. I tell them this. They laugh. They're not convinced. They keep asking questions. A rude, slippery exhilaration shoots out of me, a bubbling life force. Laughter comes loudly and I want to swallow it away. It's like I'm on a roller coaster of emotions.

That night, I can't sleep in my high room. Pamela's first telling, 'Max is dead', her deep tiredness, her weighted voice, bashes at my brain once again. The city bounces around my walls—cars starting, headlights, brakes, shouts, horns honking, glass smashing, feet running, people yelling, sirens. In my jagged wakefulness I feel too removed from the earth, too high up in my tall concrete apartment. The energy of it is wrong. My period still hasn't come.

It's raining on my twenty-seventh birthday. My windows are opened wide. I want to hear the sky.

We go to a restaurant by the beach. There are gifts and good wine and mediocre risotto and screams and camera flashes and the thump of the surf outside. I sit quietly in it all, listening to the rain easing. When the cake comes to the table I stand and blow out the candles and announce to my mum and Simon and four of my dearest friends that I've handed in my notice at work and am going to drive out to Alice Springs and live in the Central Australian desert for a while.

There are several seconds of silence. Mum asks me, in a tone of intense reserve, exactly what I'm going to do. I say I just want to try something new, freelancing maybe. Mum says it's all very sudden and have I really thought this through. I say yes. My tone tells her this is very important to me and she can't stop me. Mum asks me to consider staying at her place for a couple of weeks before I go. She says please. She says she wants to see me before she loses me for a very long time again. She says my grandmother would want it too. And my brother. Simon says, come on Finny, be a sport. I tell myself I have to be a little less selfish when it comes to my mother, I have to see her more. I smile at her and say okay.

As the chatter and questions come back to our table I excuse myself and walk through the vibrating room and go outside to great gulps of clean night air and space, and I think to myself that grief has given me clarity and I feel a core of rightness and calmness deep in me. Some decisions in life, just like love, can come surely and swiftly. And rescue just as swiftly. It just takes courage to act on them.

We drive home to Alice Springs in the rain. The creeks have come up fast. They're over the road and I drop down to first and power through the swift, soft brown water. I feel a tugging at my car's underbelly but I keep my steady course.

"You're better at this than me," says Rick grinning from the passenger seat.

Rick got me out of the still white room in Mum's house in the city and got me into the desert. I would've done it anyway, but I went with Mum's blessing with a man beside me. Rick honked the horn and drove us out of Sydney until we'd hit the mountains and then we stopped at a servo and I took over from there. I told him I was driving into the desert and I told him he could get out at any time. He didn't. I drove west into a difficult freedom.

The desert's my home now. Red dust is strong on my feet. I'm doing what I want to do. Writing. Living the dream I gave up so long ago. It's a spare kind of life and it's a glittering loneliness when Rick isn't around. He keeps on visiting. I don't love him. I can't, not yet. Through my eyes I'm showing Max the red desert. The desert that he never got to.

Rick's a good mate. He's not sure what he's going to do now that Antarctica's over for him. He saved up a lot of money in his years down there. I tell him to go overseas but I'm glad when he says he wants to stick around Alice for a while. He tells me he's never been inside Australia before. He likes it. We make an odd pair. He gets cross when I forget and call him Dip. He says we're in the real world now and it's different. He doesn't dare read his porn mags around me. And I'm trying not to swear in front of him. It was strange to see him in a T-shirt and shorts for the first time. When he first saw me again, he said I'd grown taller.

I drive through the rain and the creeks back to Alice. A small white rock is in the cassette tray by the gears. I think of this morning. The red dust like cinnamon in my cup, the splinter in my finger and the heat. Heat soaked into the sheets of my swag and heat in my toothpaste and heat in the blood that has finally come from between my legs.

The windscreen wipers swish furiously, pushing aside the strong splats.

'It's fantastic to see the rain again,' says Rick. 'Washing everything away.'

'Yeah.'

Cleave

Snip Freeman is a painter with a waitressing problem, a wanderer in search of her past. She'll visit a place, find a man and a studio and a scrap job, until the zing of uncertainty pulls her on. She is anchored nowhere, touches the earth lightly. Then she turns her back on a drowning man. And suddenly she has a reason to stay put . . .

Taking up *Shiver*'s theme of women in tough places, *Cleave* illuminates the troubled relationship between wandering and settling, belonging and freedom, parents and children, partners and lovers; between white Australia and black Australia, secretive silences and the truth. It is a novel of great power and lyricism.

'Her inimitable, urgent and demanding style makes her books impossible to put down or forget.' *Madame Figaro* (Paris)

'Nikki Gemmell lobs emotional depth charges.' *The Australian*

'Like a road movie, the novels of Nikki Gemmell capture the untamed taste of freedom.' *Le Figaro Litteraire* (France)

'A narrative style [that is] compelling and exotic.' *Baltimore Sun* (US)

'Her mastery of an epic, Odyssean style ensures that hers is one of the few truly original voices to emerge in a long time.' *Time Out* (New York)

Love Song

I'm twenty-one, it's the law, I'm twenty-one, I'm shouting it to my parents and then it stops and a tense quiet hovers in the waiting house.

Am I to die in this place, I've written in my journal on that blunted birthday, before my life has even begun?

This is the story of Lillie Bird, a woman from a locked religious community who one day finds herself in the freedom of a strange new world, England, accused of murdering a man.

But it was here, in this land of cold, dark skies and scuffed and tumbling streets that she had first found the pleasure and the sadness, and the love she had, for years, so desperately sought.

Love Song is at once a celebration of the human spirit and a powerful story of exile, identity and love. Mesmerising and heartbreaking, this is Nikki Gemmell's finest work to date.

'A striking and memorable work . . . *Love Song* will reward a second reading with pleasure in its vigour and love for life and language.' *Australian Book Review*

'I found myself caught up in the intensity of the novel, so that the act of reading was more like a strange sort of haunting than just following a narrative. It is not like any other piece of fiction I've encountered recently . . . The writing – the language, the sentence organisation, the visionary emphasis – is brilliant . . .' Peter Porter

'The energy and lust for life imbuing the work of this young Australian, and the spirit with which she inspires her heroines, is at once impetuous and caressing, devastating and full of hope.' *Le Monde*

'. . . spirited and spiritual, undershot with mordant wit and an aching moodiness.' *The Weekend Australian*